FALLEN FEATHERS

THE DEVIL'S DEAL

ELIZA RAINE

Editor: Dayna Hart

Cover: Ana Cruz

For those who struggle to believe.
Never give up.

ONE

BETH

"No. Freaking. Way. How did I ever not know this was here?"

I gaped between Nox and the mind-numbing sight before me.

Covent Garden, London.

But not as I had *ever* seen it before. The former fruit-and-vegetable market was a popular tourist spot, and it had wowed me when I had first come to London. The stylish, old, glass-covered structure was filled with cafes, bars and shops, and in the large sunken central area there was occasionally a craft market during the day, or a band playing live music at night.

But now that I could see behind the Veil...

The building still had its teal-colored metal struts that held up the glass roof, and it still had its mezzanine row of shops overlooking the lower level, where I was currently standing. Only, now I could see through the solid ground beneath my feet, to what was *under* the ancient marketplace.

The teal struts extended deep into the earth below, framing something my mind instinctively named a bazaar.

A magical-as-hell bazaar.

As many shops, cafes, and bars as there were above ground seemed to occupy the space below, and everything was lit by the warm and constantly moving glow of fairy lights - similar to the ones on Nox's deck.

I could see scores of people moving between shops, drinking with friends, or standing at tiny stalls trying to sell their goods. I couldn't hear anything, or make out any of the items they were selling, but I could see one thing clearly.

Hardly anybody down there looked human.

There were folk glowing, folk covered in fur, folk with porcelain white skin, folk with green scales, folk with an indeterminate number of limbs; my mind couldn't keep up with the parade of non-human wonderment. I saw something new every second I stared.

"It's a larger market than the human one we're standing in. It extends quite a way under the city."

I glanced at Nox as he spoke. "You said it's called Solum, right?"

He nodded. "It's the epicenter of magic in London. And it's where we'll find the one being who can tell me what the fuck is going on with my curse." His voice became a growl, and discomfort settled back over me, forcing out some of my awe.

We weren't at Covent Garden—or Solum—as tourists, I remembered reluctantly. We were trying to find out why I'd gone to bed human and woken up with wings.

Nox pushed open the door of a tiny bookstore and paused to hold it open for me. I stepped through and immediately felt a sense of quiet calm. I wondered briefly if books did that to everyone, or whether it was just me, but as soon as Nox followed me in, his presence in the tiny space dispelled the calm.

He strode past the little counter, where an old woman took a step back in alarm.

So it wasn't just me who was picking up the god of sin's foul mood.

I swallowed as I followed him to the back of the shop. He wasn't exactly being cold to me, but a barrier of some sort had definitely gone up between us. I was trying not to feel hurt or indignant about that, but it wasn't easy. I had as little idea as he did why the best night of my life had been followed by me apparently losing my humanity. In fact, I probably had even less of an idea than he did, given I knew jack-shit about magic.

But I could sort of understand why he might have become suspicious of me, so I was determined to keep my mouth shut until we knew more. He brought me with him to this place, so it wasn't like he suddenly didn't trust me at all. Unless he thought he had best keep his enemies close...

I took a long breath as he scanned the shelves, looking for something. The old lady coughed and said, "Top shelf, on the right," quietly. Nox grunted and moved his gaze to where she had directed.

Once we knew more, he would talk to me. Wouldn't he?

I had nothing to hide, and no agenda. There was no reason for him not to trust me, and whomever we were going to visit should only confirm that.

His words rang through my mind. *"I don't think you're human anymore."*

It hadn't seemed to occur to him that those words might freak me out more than him. He'd done little in the way of reassuring me, and a lot in the way of brooding angrily in the hour it had taken us to dress and get to Covent Garden. Which wasn't the ideal way to follow a night of passion. I'd hoped for waffles and coffee and flirtatious groping. Not trying to deal with the idea of not being human.

I didn't really believe that. At all.

I figured that's why I was more anxious about the new tension between Nox and I than the faint wings I had seen on my back.

I was guessing they were connected to Nox's curse. After all, *I* was, somehow. And Nox was powerful and magical. He would be able to handle whatever was happening.

He radiated power, and every nerve in my body

longed for him. Longed for his strength, his power, his touch, the pleasure he could create.

A realization dawned on me slowly as I stared at his broad back.

I wanted him so much that my biggest fear was never feeling that touch again, rather than finding out I wasn't human. Surely that wasn't right?

I gave myself a mental slap as he reached for a book on the shelf. *Sort it out Beth. Get your damn priorities straight. Wings before sex.*

"Introitus," Nox muttered, turning over the book he'd plucked off the shelf. I peered at it. War and Peace. Huh.

My eyes widened as the bookcase in front of us shimmered and then faded completely, revealing a stone staircase lit by hundreds of the little, floating fairy-lights.

Nox put the book back on one of the still-solid shelves and looked at me. "I'll go ahead, if you don't mind."

His awkwardly formal words were at least spoken in a warm, reassuring tone, and I nodded.

"Sure."

"There is much to see, but it is imperative we make our way straight to Adstutus. You will have plenty of time to explore Solum at a later date."

"Right," I nodded again. "No getting distracted. Got it."

TWO

BETH

I did my best to focus on Nox as he led me through the bazaar. There was so much to see on either side of me that I could feel my senses becoming overwhelmed.

Smells of coffee and spices flowed around me, and the languages I could hear being spoken were totally alien. Every time I paused, agog at a table of wares that looked like they'd come from outer space, Nox would get too far ahead of me, and panic forced my legs to hurry after him. God only knew what would happen if I got lost in the chaos.

I had expected it to feel claustrophobic, being so crowded and underground, but it wasn't at all. It was weirdly open and cool, and plenty of warm light flowed from the millions of tiny dancing lights around us.

"Answer all of Adstutus' questions honestly," Nox said as I fell into stride next to him.

I bristled, my resolve to stay neutral until we found

out what was happening crumbling at the insinuation that I would lie. "I'm always honest," I snapped.

Nox glanced sideways at me, his blue eyes bright. A smile pulled the corner of his mouth for the first time since we'd left his bed. "Yes. I think you probably are."

"Who is Adstutus?" I asked, stumbling a bit on the pronunciation. "And why will he know more about this than you do? Is he more powerful?" I knew asking if someone was more powerful than he was would make Nox bristle in return, and that's why I did it. His shoulders squared.

"He's not as powerful as me, but he is much, much older. And very knowledgeable."

"Have you talked to him about your curse before?"

"Yes. He suggested that I can only break it by collecting the sins back."

I stepped to the side in surprise as a man with blue skin shot an arm out in front of me, waving some cooked meat on a stick and grinning wildly. Nox glared at him as we passed and he slunk away, grin falling.

"Is Adstutus a fallen angel too?" I asked as we rounded a bend into a quieter area, with lots stores that had painted glass windows with little canvas canopies.

"No. He's a genie."

I opened my mouth, then closed it again. If he bore any resemblance whatsoever to a large blue balloon, or sounded a hint like Robin Williams, I would be forced to question my sanity. Again.

Nox angled for one of the stores and I scanned the writing on the window. *Alchemy and Cures.*

. . .

Stepping into the room behind the glass was like stepping into another world. Gentle chimes played into the soft space, the music soaked up by the huge colorful rugs hanging on the walls. Low shelving units held gold jars and dozens of bowls and bottles filled with bright powders. Something that looked remarkably like a stone well stood in the middle of the room, the sound of bubbling water mingling with the chimes. Carvings of camels and dunes and palm trees covered the well, solidifying the Arabic vibe the store was giving. The scent of peppermint wafted over me and a man popped into existence before us.

I bit down on my startled curse as he bowed his head. "Mr. Nox. What a pleasure."

The baggy golden harem pants and long black beard he wore kind of fit in with the shop. The Metallica t-shirt and tattooed skull on his bald head, however, did not.

"Adstutus. Thank you for seeing me at short notice."

"I wasn't aware I had a choice." The genie smiled, but his expression was loaded with sarcasm.

"You're right, you don't." Nox's voice was hard.

"Then let us dispense with the pleasantries, shall we? What do you need?" His gaze focused on me, and interest flickered in his dark eyes. "Who is this?"

Nox stepped close beside me and warmth wrapped itself around my body. The protective gesture buoyed me. "I'm Beth," I said.

"And tell me, Beth, what are you?"

loved that movie," I said.

"The book is better."

"Really?"

"Yeah. But I love both."

"I'm Beth," I said, moving between the desks toward him. He shot a hand up.

"Close enough, Beth. Take a seat there." A little surprised, I pulled a chair toward me and sat down. He smiled at me. "From what I've heard, the Boss is keen on you, and I don't think he'd be too impressed if I bit you."

"Bit me?" My heart hammered fast in my chest.

"I see Rory prepped you well," he grinned. "I'm a vampire. No bright lights, and no coming close enough for me to hear your heartbeat. Just remember those two rules, and we'll get along just fine, Beth."

SIX

BETH

A vampire.

My new colleague was a vampire, and nobody, including Nox, thought to mention this to me before I met him.

I swallowed as I studied his pale face with new apprehension.

His smile faltered a little. "I'm guessing you're new to the Veil?" I nodded. "And vampires?"

"You're my first," I confirmed.

His smile returned. "Okay. Let me just clarify a few things. I'm not a predator. I mean, I am, of course, I live on blood, but it's not a Dracula situation. I drink animal blood. No praying on innocent humans or any of that jazz."

I gave him a weak smile. "That's good to know."

"Honestly, the most remarkable thing about me is not my fangs."

I raised my eyebrows. "Dare I ask what is the most remarkable thing?"

"Hmmm, toss up between my love for dinosaurs and my ability with tech."

I glanced at the screens, then back to him. "Dinosaurs and computers are a lot easier to process for me than vampires," I said. "No offense."

"You've seen too many films," he shrugged.

"About the not coming too close thing..." I gave him a pointed look. If he wasn't dangerous why did I have to keep my distance?

"Ah. Yeah. On occasion, the sound of a human heart pumping blood can cause me to lose concentration." I took a deep breath as subtlety as I could. "But that hardly ever happens. Still, better safe than sorry. Right, are you ready for your induction?"

"Erm..." I hadn't been ready for anything that had happened to me recently. How scary was a vampire dinosaur-geek in the grand scheme of things? "Sure. Show me the ropes, Malcolm."

"Malc," he said, turning back to his keyboard. "You can call me Malc. I chose the name after Ian Malcolm from Jurassic Park."

"Oh. Cool. What's your real name?"

"Impossible to pronounce in English," he said, throwing me a grin. "That's why I picked a new one."

His smile was genuine, and I relaxed my shoulders as I pulled my notepad out of my bag. "Can you only go out at night?"

"Yes. And I only sleep about an hour a day. I'm here most of the time."

I gestured to the screens. "What are these?"

"Feeds. From all the magical hotspots in London. And a couple from abroad too. You'll have a new laptop tomorrow, and I'll load it with the software you need for the research work the Boss mentioned he wanted you to do. Library access, government documents, Ward archives, all of it."

"Ward archives?" I asked, opting to ignore the fact that I would have access to government documents. That couldn't be legal.

"Yeah." He turned back to me slowly. "You know about the Ward?"

"Erm..."

"Wow. A real newbie. Fun." He turned back and gestured to the screen. The images changed, until one picture was spread across all of them. A navy-blue logo, a capital 'W' with crossed lines on each of the outside edges of the letter and a pale lightning bolt behind it. "The Ward is in charge of everything the gods can't be bothered with. Which is pretty much everything on Earth."

"Nox said that there were five cities with magic on Earth?" My brain faltered slightly when referring to Earth like there was another place beings could exist.

"Yes. And ninety-nine percent of magical creatures stick together, because magic fuels magic. The more of us there are, the better our magic works. If we spend a lifetime away from magic completely, we'll eventually lose it. For some creatures, that means they'll die."

I scribbled in my pad. This was news to me. Nox had said that magic lasted longer if it was around other magic, but he hadn't mentioned anything about losing it completely.

"The Ward controls all of the magic that powers the Veil, keeping us hidden from non-magical people. And they have enforcers called Wardens, who make sure that those same non-magical people aren't taken advantage of. I mean they'd be freaking helpless against some of us." Red gleamed in his eyes for a second and then was gone.

"What stops the Ward from abusing their power over magic people?" I asked.

"The gods," Malc shrugged. "It's a good system. It works. Dangerous magical beings are kept in check, and the rest of us get plenty of opportunity to enjoy our gifts."

I decided I didn't want to ask how a vampire enjoyed his gifts. "Nox said something about designated Veil nights?" I said instead.

"Yeah. And places like Solum, where we can be ourselves. The Ward use their powerful magic to make all that possible."

"Right. And you?" I kept my nerves out of my voice as I looked at him. "What do you do?"

"I'm the Boss's spy. I keep an eye on everything, so he's the first to know when anything is happening in the Veil that shouldn't be. I guess he likes to be informed. He doesn't really get on with the Ward all the time."

"Why not?" I asked.

"He used to be in charge of it." Rory had alluded to that before, I remembered. "He abandoned the post abruptly, spent the next few decades wreaking havoc, and they were never able to prove it was him. He was too powerful, and too smart, to ever get caught." Malc threw me another grin. "He's a bit of a legend, to be honest."

"He's the devil. You don't get much more legendary than that," I mumbled. I could easily imagine Nox causing lust-, greed-, and gluttony-fueled chaos all over London in the sixties and seventies. And a weird part of me wished I'd had been there to see it.

"Well, he's less fun now than he used to be. Now he co-operates with them and they leave him alone. But that hasn't stopped him keeping an eye on things. Via me." He gestured proudly at his screens and they updated again, each showing footage of a different place. I recognized at least three as Solum. "And my current job is to look for anyone who might be buying or selling pages of sin, and tracking down the fallen angels who took them."

"Do you often find lost people for him?"

"Sure. Magical people are very good at hiding though, so it's not always easy. Nor are these fucking bits of paper he needs back, either, though." He peered at me suddenly, red eyes interested. "Why, have you lost someone?"

I opened my mouth to tell him, but guilt made me close it again. I had agreed with Nox that we would find his lost sins first. It wasn't right to bring up my parents within an hour of starting the job.

I shrugged. "It can wait. So, Nox knows who he gave his sins to, right?"

"Right," Malc said, and held up his hand, counting down on his fingers as he spoke. "He gave Wrath to Madaleine, but she sold her page. The guy he gave Sloth to vanished ages ago. We know Pride went to Singapore, and I'm currently scouring everything we have to find out what he's doing there. And Envy is a big social media star, but we don't know where she actually lives. She's super good at hiding all trails that might lead us to her, and even I can't get through her online defenses. We have a whole team of hackers with dubious backgrounds working on it now."

"Have you tried sending her a message?"

Malc gave me a look. "Yes. We get the same response, daily. *Fuck off.*"

"Oh. Do you think they all still have their pages and only Madaleine sold hers?"

"We don't know."

"So, how can I help?"

"You can start looking through the transactions from all the pawn brokers and blackmarket dealers that we have info for, and flag up anything interesting."

I nodded. It didn't sound exciting, but it did sound useful.

"And don't worry, you're not expected to work in a dark room all day. Nox had the office next door set up for you. And I'll be on video link most of the time, so you won't be on your own all the time."

I smiled, relieved. Sitting in the dark for hours at a

time wasn't really my idea of a great working environment. "Okay. So what shall I-"

"Ooooh, hold on, got something coming in." Malc spun his chair away from me, fingers flying over the keyboard as pinging noises sounded. "It's serious. A murder. A supernatural murder..."

The screens changed, and I saw grainy CCTV footage outside an apartment block that looked like it was in one of the rougher parts of the city.

Sound filtered through the room suddenly, and I realized it was police talking on radios.

"No, he's definitely dead," said a female voice. "No need for an ambulance."

"How do you know it's a supernatural murder?" I asked, a gruesome part of me interested. It felt more like TV show than something actually happening somewhere in London.

"I'm tuned into Ward radios," Malc said, eyebrows wiggling mischievously. "Those are Wardens talking."

The static radio crackling hissed, then the female voice came through again. "...distinct magical residue reported. No, we need someone experienced please."

There was a pause, then a male voice replied. "Banks here. Description, please."

"Human male, throat ripped out. Likely shifter work, except the magical residue is too strong."

My interest waned as my mind created a gory visual to go with the woman's words. This was real. Not a TV show. A man had had his throat ripped out. I started to move, about to make an excuse about needing to use the restroom, when the male voice answered.

"Right. I'll be there shortly. Do we know who the victim is?"

"Yes. An Alex Smith."

I felt the blood drain from my face.

My ex was named Alex Smith.

And he had been on the run from wolves when I'd last closed my door on him.

SEVEN

BETH

B ile rose in my throat, an acidic burn moving from my stomach all the way through my body, as I stared down at the bloodstained floor.

It was Alex's blood.

All over the already disgusting carpet, all over the faded couch, all the over the dirty walls.

He was dead. The man I had shared a short, but important part of my life with, was dead.

"Beth? Do you want to leave?" Nox's voice was quiet but forceful, snapping my focus to him as he touched my elbow.

I shook my head, unwilling to open my mouth. The metallic stench of the blood was strong enough that I was convinced I would taste it if I did. More nausea pulled at me, but the dizziness I'd experienced on finding Sarah's body was strangely absent.

Nox had brought us here the moment Malc had told

him about it. And there had been no question that it was Alex. My Alex. My *ex* Alex.

He may have been a giant asshole, but I was certain that he hadn't deserved... whatever the hell had caused this much blood.

Heat burned at the back of my eyes. I wasn't upset about losing him. I'd had no intention of ever seeing the man again. But the thought of him suffering was still distressing.

"Miss Abbott, Mr. Nox." A man stepped in front of us, and I concentrated on him. There were plenty of police officers in the tiny apartment, and people in white shellsuits who had been wheeling a bodybag out when we had arrived. But this man was one of only two in a normal suit and tie. He had warm brown eyes that seemed to carry genuine sorrow at the situation, and tidy hair to go with his neatly trimmed beard.

"I'm Banks, and I'm with the Ward." He spoke to Nox, throwing regular, reassuring glances at me. I must have looked as shaken as I felt. "An Inspector Singh with the human homicide police will be here shortly, and I will be liaising with her on this."

"It's a supernatural killing, then?" Nox's voice was deep and laced with a power that stood out against the conciliatory tone of the Warden.

"Yes. A strong magical residue was detected here."

"I sense nothing," Nox said.

"It faded fast. We have sprites who check all murders in London within moments of our awareness of them, and there was something powerful here before he was killed."

"Not a shifter?"

"No. Why?" Banks narrowed his eyes slightly at Nox. He would have no idea that we had heard him on the radio earlier, if Malc's hacking was as effective as he claimed it was.

"I heard someone say his throat had been ripped out."

"And last time I saw him, he said he was being chased by wolves." My voice came out hoarse, but at least it was audible. "I turned him away."

Banks focused on me. "You're his ex-girlfriend?"

I nodded. "Yes. We didn't part on good terms. He stole my TV."

"Did you know he was living here?"

"No. The last time I saw him he asked if he could stay with me. To hide from the wolves chasing him. I think the Veil had been lifted for him and he was starting to see magic. He was... a mess. Scared." I swallowed, as more guilt and sadness gripped me. "Do you think he suffered?" I couldn't help the wobble in my voice as I asked the question.

"No," Banks said gently. "If his throat was removed he would have died very quickly."

A silent tear escaped, and I gave up trying to stop any others from following it. "Good. I didn't like him, but I didn't wish him dead."

"Banks! Human copper here for you!" yelled a voice from the door.

"Excuse me a minute. I have a few more questions, do you mind waiting?"

"We'll be here," Nox answered for me.

I turned away from the blood as Banks made his way out of the apartment, trying to look at anything else. A tiny kitchen was on the opposite wall, and an open door beside it showed a bedroom that looked like a tornado had torn through it.

"Has someone been searching for something or was he an untidy person?" Nox asked quietly. He was standing close, but not reaching out to touch or comfort me, and I was grateful. If he hugged me, the tears would come faster.

Plus, Nox was the new guy in my life, even if it was complicated as hell. It didn't seem right to embrace him in my dead ex's home.

"I guess he didn't do any tidying at mine, so he might have lived like this if he was on his own," I shrugged, gazing around the apartment.

There were piles of stuff that were clearly not Alex's everywhere I looked. Stacks of DVDs littered the floor, and the kitchen counter had what looked like dozens of small jewelry boxes on it. A large bust of a bearded, shirt-less Greek god stood in front of a bookshelf that was full of cellphone boxes.

"Looks like he upped his stealing game," I mumbled, moving even farther from the blood, and closer to the bedroom. Designer t-shirts were strewn about with cheap ones, and hotel robes and spa slippers lay crumpled on the floor. "Where did he get all this stuff from?"

"More like who," a female voice answered. I turned, seeing Inspector Singh with Banks. She had a slightly dazed look on her normally sharp face. "There are a number of petty thieves in this part of London that he could have been fencing stuff for."

"We don't believe this was the work of a small-time city criminal," Banks' calm voice replied. "There was powerful magic involved."

Singh scowled. "Alex Smith was not smart enough to be involved in anything more exciting than petty thievery."

"He wasn't stupid," I interjected. "Lazy and dishonest, but not stupid."

"Whatever he was involved in got him killed, by someone or something powerful, and we will get to the bottom of it," Banks said. "Now, Miss Abbott, can you tell me where you have been over the course of today?"

A sick anxiety crept up my body, and when Nox's hand closed around mine I gripped it back, my earlier apprehension about letting him comfort me in Alex's home gone. "I'm a suspect?"

"No. You have no magic. But I need the information all the same. As I will from Mr. Nox." The Warden focused on Nox, and Singh's gaze followed. I watched her eyes widen as a slow, rolling heat emanated from the man standing beside me. The *fallen angel* standing beside me.

"My whereabouts are beyond your concern," Nox growled at Banks. His grip tightened around my hand, and new nerves twisted my stomach.

"We were together, this morning, in Solum," I blurted

quickly. Nox losing his shit would help nothing, and only make us look like we had something to hide.

Banks looked at me, and I could see the unease under his calm facade. Nox scared him. Hell, Nox scared everyone. "Solum?" He asked mildly.

"Yes. Nox was showing me Solum. We had coffee." I left out the visit to the genie. "Then we went back to the office."

"And you were together from then on?"

"N..no. We were working on separate floors."

"And how did you get here so fast?"

"I received a call," Nox said, in a voice laced with gravel. More heat was rippling off him, and his grip hadn't loosened. "As I am sure you are well aware, I am exceptionally well connected." The threat was clear. *Don't fuck with me.*

"Are you informed about all murders in London?" Banks' tone was innocent enough, but his insinuation was clear.

"Any that involve those connected to me or to wolves, yes." Nox's hissed answer surprised me.

"Wolves?" I asked, before I could stop myself.

"Since Alex told you he was being chased by wolves, I have been keeping a close eye on a volatile pack in North London."

"Why?" I asked at the same time as Banks.

"I do not trust them." Nox looked directly at the Warden. "I will give you the information I have on the pack. Now, we are leaving. Contact my assistant if you wish to speak to me, or Miss Abbott, again."

He turned, pulling me after him. The swathes of dark red blood were a blur in my peripherals as I was swept from the room.

I gulped down air as we got outside, making a point not to look at the ambulance Alex's body must be in.

"You should go home. Get some sleep. You've had a lot to process in a short amount of time." Nox turned to face me as he spoke, and his expression was softer than his tone.

"You're angry," I said. It wasn't really what I meant to say, but the words came out.

Still clutching my left hand in his right, he lifted his other and wiped an almost dried tear from my cheek. "Yes."

"Why?"

"Many reasons. I don't like to see you cry. I don't like the suggestion that I had anything to do with this. I don't like Banks." He paused, and light flared in his piercing eyes. "And I don't like the thought of you with anyone else."

I blinked. "Really?"

"Yes." A primal edge took his voice, but his eyes softened before they could turn fully feral. "This is not the place, or time," he muttered, and I got the feeling he was talking to himself, rather than me.

"I haven't loved Alex in a long time," I said quietly. "Not really. But it's not easy seeing this."

"I know. Go home. Claude will take you. If you want

to work tomorrow, I will see you then. If not, I understand."

I nodded. He was right. I did need some time alone.

My apartment felt odd as I stepped inside. Odd in a good way, I supposed. I put my purse down carefully on the counter and made my way to the fridge to search for wine.

Glass in hand, I slumped on the couch and stared at the place the TV used to be. It was a strange reminder of Alex, and my throat constricted.

I meant what I'd said to Nox, I hadn't loved him in a long time. But he had been my friend, companion, and a constant presence in my life for a significant amount of time, and although a hell of a lot had happened since I asked him to move out, it really wasn't very long ago.

I took a long sip of wine, closed my eyes, and leaned my head back. I needed to acknowledge the horrible thought lurking at the back of my mind, pulling at me. Deciding to face it, I let the question fill my head.

Had Alex been introduced to the Veil and magic and maybe wolves, because of me?

Was he dead because of me?

He'd been sleeping with Sarah, somebody with magic, for months before I knew about it, I reminded myself firmly. I felt my grip on the wine glass tighten as I thought about that fact, and took a deep breath.

His apartment was full of stolen shit, and I didn't know any wolves at all.

I had nothing to do with the Veil being lifted for him.

Alex got himself into whatever it was that had gotten him killed. Not me.

I repeated the thought out loud, sitting up straight and opening my eyes.

"Alex got himself killed. It wasn't my fault."

I nodded, and took another drink.

"Nothing changes. Find the sins, lift Nox's curse, find my parents. Don't have sex and accidentally steal devil power that you can't use."

Shit.

How many times would I end up questioning the craziness of my life, now that Nox was a part of it?

Thinking about him made me take another gulp of wine.

Every part of me knew he was dangerous, on an innate level. The hint of possessiveness he'd shown earlier had surprised me. He had been as possessive as it was possible to be during the night we'd spent together, but for some reason, I hadn't expected that outside of the bedroom. I wondered if that was because part of me was still convinced he would tire of me, or lose interest now he had gotten what he wanted.

But he hadn't lost interest yet.

Was that because I was his only option?

Why, why, why was I the only person he could be with?

I groaned, flopping backward and nearly spilling my drink.

I'd been wondering the same thing for days, and the genie didn't know, Nox didn't know, nobody knew. Maybe Nox's god, Examinus, might know, but Nox sure as hell wasn't going to ask him.

I forced myself to picture my parents' faces. Hope flickered to life inside me, brightening everything, forcing the darker thoughts I usually associated with them to recede into the shadows.

I finally had a chance to find them. I had to focus on that.

EIGHT

BETH

My first thought the next day, when I woke from an uneasy sleep, was the blood splattered all over Alex's apartment. The image stuck with me while I showered, and no matter how hard I scrubbed, I felt restless and dirty somehow.

I had woken far earlier than I usually did, and soon found myself with rubber gloves and bleach in my hands. I set about cleaning everything in my apartment from top to bottom, as though making my own place spotless would erase the awfulness of Alex's apartment.

Every single surface was sparkling by the time I had to leave for work, but the uneasy sense hadn't lessened.

"Morning, Malc," I said as I entered what I found myself thinking of as his lair, rather than his office.

"Not morning for me," he grinned. I'd been careful

this time with the door, knocking and then shutting it quickly behind me.

"Oh." A thought occurred to me. "Do vampires drink coffee?"

"Nope."

"Okay."

"So. You had a busy evening." His lively eyes fixed on mine.

"Alex Smith is my ex-boyfriend," I said. He would already know that, but I felt like I should get it out there early.

"You know, I don't think it was wolves."

"Really?"

Malc shook his head enthusiastically. "There is no way they'd send Banks if it was shifters. Unless it's a bigass shifter, with megapower."

"Is Banks a big deal then?" Nerves made me fidget in my seat. Singh thinking I was guilty of murder had been bad enough. A hot-shot supernatural cop's scrutiny would be worse. *Nobody thinks you did it this time,* I told myself. *You don't have magic.*

"He's been around a while. And he moves cities, which most supernaturals don't."

"Does Nox know him?" I had assumed not, but his comment about disliking Banks would make more sense if he did.

"He'll know *of* him." Malc shrugged. "I don't know if they've met before. Like I said, the Boss tends to stay out of Ward business these days. So, wanna go to your office and start tracking down this lost book? I'll video call you in ten."

I hadn't actually been in the office next door that had been allocated to me, and I was relieved when I pushed open the door and saw light flooding in.

Lots of light. The room was small, only big enough for a desk down the middle and a chair on each side, but the far wall was all glass. I stepped up to it and stared out over the river. The gleaming form of The Shard made all the other massive glass buildings look tiny.

"This is awesome," I breathed aloud. I mean, the view from my old floor was good if you went up to the glass, but I'd never been given my own room to stare out at it from before. Somehow it felt like my own personal view.

With the calmest sigh I'd managed in in a while, I turned back to the desk. A laptop was plugged into a monitor, and I sat down in front of it.

As soon as I was logged on, and invitation to a video call popped up.

"All set up? Looks bright in there."

I smiled at Malc's face on the screen. "It is bright. I like it."

"Good. Right, now in your menu you'll see a program called Tidaction. Open it up. The search engine on this is a little old school, and slow as hell, so you'll have to be patient with it."

I went through the steps as he talked me through

each of the programs on the new laptop, making notes on which one was best for different types of information and all the common issues. He was a good teacher, enthusiastic and engaged, and I only got him to pause once, so that I could top up with coffee and use the restroom. By lunchtime, I had a pretty basic idea of the technology, and I was starting to get excited about playing detective.

"So," I said, swallowing a large bite of ham sandwich. "You said I should start by searching pawnbrokers and black market dealers?"

"Yeah. For anything book-related, or sheet-of-paper related. Then you can use the other programs to search for whatever the dealer claimed to have sold. See if it looks right or not."

I nodded. "Do you think anyone would be likely to sell the book?"

Malc snorted, confirming that he was thinking the same as I was. "Nobody is risking stealing the fucking book of sins from the devil, just to sell it."

"What do you think they want it for, then?"

"It can't be anything good," he replied.

I thought about what Nox had said about his brothers plotting against him. "Maybe it's one of the people who got one of the sins, who doesn't want to give it back." That made the most sense to me.

"They're not people, Beth. They're fallen angels, and they're powerful as fuck. Do you mind me swearing?" He raised his pale eyebrows and peered at me through the camera. I couldn't help a chuckle.

"No. Tell me more about the book. Did the gods give

it to Nox?"

"No, Nox made it himself."

"Oh. Why?"

"I don't know. I just know the book is almost as old as he is."

A thought occurred to me. "How old are you, Malc?"

"A hundred and six."

I nodded, trying to hide my intake of breath. There were definitely some things about the Veil that would take me some time to get used to. Maybe watching special effects movies and TV all my life made the people with blue skin or wings easier to accept than things like someone who looked and sounded my age being over a hundred years old.

"Cool," I said. Malc flashed me a mischievous look, before typing furiously on his keyboard.

"I'll let you get on with the pawnbrokers. Let me know if you have any problems with anything."

"Thanks."

I spent all afternoon lost in lists of transactions, and looking up anything that sounded like it could be a sin page of the devil's book in disguise. A number of times I had to stop myself from getting caught up in reading about artifacts or books that sounded beyond belief - like a book that caused houses to burn down, and a scroll that tried to eat souls.

My phone rang at nearly five, and my heart did a little flutter as I saw Nox's number.

"Hi," I said as I answered the call.

"Banks and Singh are in my office. They would like to speak to us."

My elation plummeted. "I'll be right up."

NINE

BETH

The second I saw Nox, my body, and maybe some subconscious part of my brain, realized I had been away from him for more than twelve hours and abruptly couldn't stand that fact.

My legs propelled me toward him, heat swirling from my chest through my whole body. His eyes blazed with light, hunger playing across his face as he stood up, his huge desk between us.

"Miss Abbott."

I stopped moving, taking in the rest of the room.

"Mr. Banks," I acknowledged awkwardly as he stood and extended his hand to me.

"Warden Banks," he corrected, with a smile. It wasn't one of those intimidating, or condescending smiles, so I smiled back and shook his hand.

"Sure. Sorry."

"I'd hoped not to come back here," sighed Singh. I

turned to see her examining Nox's bookshelf. "Hello, Miss Abbott."

"Hello, Inspector."

"Ask your questions," said Nox, cutting off any avenue for small talk. He looked pissed, I realized as I focused on him with the part of my brain that wasn't wired directly to my lady-bits.

"Okay then. I need more detail about where you were the day of the murder," Banks said, sitting back down in the guest chair. Singh came to stand behind him, and I hovered unsurely in the middle.

"As Beth told you, we were in Solum in the morning, and here in the afternoon."

"Who were you with in the afternoon?" Banks asked.

"Rory." There was a strain to Nox's voice that suggested even the clipped answers he was giving were a struggle to keep polite.

"We'll need to talk with her."

"Fine. Inspector Singh won't be able to, though, she's a pixie."

Singh started to say something, then seemed to think better of it and closed her mouth.

"What is the nature of your relationship with Miss Abbott?" Banks asked the question so calmly, I had to admire him. With Nox staring me down like he was about to erupt, I would be nervous as hell.

"I don't see how that is relevant to anything."

"Please, Mr. Nox. I don't want to be here any more than you want me to be. But you must understand why I am."

Nox snarled, an actual animal sound, and both Singh and I stepped backward. "I challenge you to find a single throat that didn't deserve my attention," Nox barked.

"Mr. Nox, please. I am certainly not here to challenge you." I flicked my eyes between the men, trying to work out if that was true. Was he challenging Nox? Or just doing his job?

"Answer my questions, and I will leave you in peace."

I envied his calm. My heart was hammering in my chest. I had no idea what throats they were talking about, and wasn't sure I wanted to know, but it had tipped Nox into fill-the-room-with-scary-as-hell-magic mode. Even just a tiny bit of loss of control by the devil was terrifying.

"Miss Abbott is my employee and close friend."

My middle constricted, a nasty icy feeling adding to the hot anxiety. What did that even mean? *Employee and close friend?*

"Had you engaged with Alex Smith in any way prior to his murder?"

Shadows billowed suddenly from Nox's back, gone almost as fast as they appeared. "I did not engage with him at all. I have never spoken with the man."

"You had a theft recently."

"That has nothing to do with you."

The heat was becoming unbearable, and I pulled uncomfortably at my top, wishing my pulse would slow down. I glanced at Singh, who looked equally as uncomfortable, and appeared to have moved closer to the door.

Banks cleared his throat. "Max knew Alex."

At the name of the man who had tried to kill me a

short time ago, my heart rate kicked up another notch. "Max mentioned Alex," I spluttered. "He was jealous because he was..." I trailed off unwilling to say *sleeping with Sarah*.

Banks nodded. "I am afraid, Mr. Nox, that you and Miss Abbott have a rather a lot of connections to the victim. May we speak to your assistant now?"

"You may. This way, please." Rory's annoyed voice came from the doorway, and everyone except Singh looked up at her.

Banks looked back at Nox, standing rigid as a statue. "Thank you for your time. We'll be in touch."

As soon as the police were out of the door, Singh looking distinctly relieved to be leaving, heat engulfed the room.

"Nox," I started, turning to him just as his whole arm burst into flames.

I yelped, stumbling backward as his fist slammed down into his beautiful wooden desk.

Shadows had covered his normally electric-blue irises and his wings were spreading out behind him, inky darkness swirling across the gleaming gold.

"Nox," I breathed again, both terrified and mesmerized by the flaming angel before me.

"That man is not welcome here." His voice was raw and filled with power.

"Talk to me," I said, my own voice barely more than a whisper. "And please, can you make it less hot."

His black eyes focused on mine, and the shadows began to leak away, bright blue flaring to life instead.

The flames burning across his shirt sputtered out and the heat lessened. He kept his searing gaze on mine as I took a deep breath of cooler air. "Talk to me," I said again, my voice stronger. "Why are you so angry?"

"He thinks I killed him."

"Why? Why does he think that?" I was half-scared to ask, but I had to.

Heat swelled again, but I kept my eyes locked on his even as I saw flames rise from his chest in my peripheral vision.

"You do not know the real me, Beth. You know the man I am now."

My heart beat even harder and I felt a little dizzy. "Did you kill Alex?" I knew the answer was no. I knew it for certain. But I needed to get my point across to him.

"Of course not," he growled.

"Then the man you are now is all that I am interested in." The returning shadows halted. The flames died down, fading from view. "The man I spent the night with is the man standing before me now. You told me right at the start who you were. I have seen a glimpse of what you are capable of." I swallowed. I knew what he wanted to hear, what I should say to him, but I wasn't sure if I really meant the words I was about to say.

I said them anyway.

"I can handle it."

His jaw clenched so tight I thought his teeth might crack.

I took a step closer to him.

"Nox, I can handle it."

"That isn't the point! You do not deserve this!" I flinched as he shouted, but stood my ground. "Beth, you are light, and I am dark. You are good and I deal in evil. I do not want you to hear about the worst parts of me. Do you understand?"

I nodded. And I did understand. I wouldn't want the worst things about myself exposed to him either. And I wasn't the damn devil.

"Then we won't talk about it. We'll find the real murderer, and get on with lifting your curse."

More blue light filled his eyes as his expression softened. "If we lift my curse, we will be forced to talk about it."

"Then we'll talk then. Not now."

He tilted his head, then let out a long breath. "I missed you."

My heart swelled at his words, and some of the tension gripping me lessened.

"I missed you too. I didn't realize how much, until I saw you." I allowed my eyes to roam from his, and realized he'd burned most of his shirt off. The adrenaline already buzzing through my system ramped up as I took in his bare chest.

"Please, sit down," he said, an awkward formality to his tone.

No sex, no sex, no sex. Formal was best, I reminded myself.

"Do you know Banks?" I asked, taking a seat. I felt

myself relax a touch as my slightly trembly knees got a break.

Nox had turned to a unit behind him and was taking out a shirt on hanger. Maybe he made a habit of burning his shirts off in a temper.

"No. But I have history with the Ward. They do not like me."

I decided honesty was the best policy and answered him truthfully. "I know. Malc told me a bit about it."

"I'm sure he gave you a colorful version," Nox muttered. I watched as he discarded the remains of his old shirt and began pulling on the new one. The way his naked, muscular shoulders moved made me believe that swooning was a real thing.

"I don't mean to tell you what to do or anything," I said slowly. "But it might make our lives easier if you don't lose it every time they talk to us. I mean... I was living with Alex up until recently, and he had a connection to another murder that we were involved in. You can sort of see why they need to talk to us."

Nox paused with his back to me for a long moment and then turned to face me, shirt hanging open.

I crossed my legs.

"I believe that your suggestion of taking action ourselves will help me contain my annoyance."

"Good," I said.

"And I have a lead on one of the sins."

I sat up straight. "Really?"

"Madaleine called. She claims to know where Sloth is. We are to meet her tonight at one of my casinos."

TEN

BETH

Unsurprisingly, casinos were not a place I frequented. I didn't have enough money to lose to be risking it on black or red.

When I got out of the car and saw just how imposing the Provoco Casino was, I knew immediately that I was underdressed. It was not one of those places that had neon signs for slot machines in the windows.

It dominated an entire corner of Cranbourn Street, and a massive, thirties-era glass awning covered the huge entrance.

We ascended the polished steps, and two well-dressed men opened the door for us.

All the people milling about in the grand lobby were wearing either floor-length gowns, or very short sexy dresses. Everywhere I looked were tuxedos and jewelry.

I was wearing what I had worn to the office that day.

Nox looked impeccable as usual in a navy suit.

People nodded respectfully to him as he strode past, and I wondered if he even noticed it anymore.

The place oozed wealth. Smartly dressed croupiers were standing on the glossy tiles behind dozens of gambling tables, and punters were moving large stacks of brightly colored chips around as though they were nothing. I wasn't sure what I had expected when Nox said we were visiting a casino, but it was less 'slot machine chimes and drunk people cheering', and more 'Monte Carlo opulence'.

"Didn't you say you lose all your money every night because you kept Greed?" I asked Nox quietly.

"Yes. I have lots of companies I passed on ownership for, so that all the money isn't lost, and those owners pay me daily."

"Huh. So you don't technically own this place?"

"Not technically, no." His words said one thing, and his tone said the complete opposite. He was as much the boss here as he was at LMS, regardless of whose name was on the paperwork, I guessed.

When we reached the other side of the casino floor, a man in a suit opened a door for us. "What would you like to drink, sir?" he asked.

"My usual whiskey. And the lady will have a French 75."

"That's the champagne one, right?" I whispered as I followed him through the door.

"Yes. I remember that you liked it?" He looked at me, suave confidence on his face.

The feminist in me longed to tell him I'd order my

own drinks, thank you very much. The rest of me knew that he was absolutely right, I did love it, and I'd never have had the guts to order it myself.

"Yes. Thank you," I said.

We had entered a room with only a few tables in it, and I realized as I looked around that the people at them were even more finely attired than those in the main building. Then my eyes settled on Madaleine, and Cornu.

She stood when she saw us, showing off the ivory dress she was only half wearing. I had always heard that you should choose either a plunging neckline or a high leg split, but she had opted for both. And if I was being honest, she looked amazing. Her white hair was in a sleek high tail, and she smiled as we approached.

"I'm glad you could make it." Cornu grinned beside her, looking sharp in a tailored black suit.

"You don't need to welcome me to my own establishment, Madaleine," Nox said. They both sat on leather stools at the felt covered table, so I did the same, feeling quite severely out of my comfort zone.

A waiter came over with our drinks, and I took mine gratefully.

"Beth, do you play?" Madaleine leaned past Nox as fixed her attention on me.

"Erm, play what?"

"Poker. Texas hold 'em."

I shook my head, and she gave a dramatic sigh. "I can't play with him." She nodded at Nox. "He can't win."

"It's true. Cursed by Greed. But I can tell Beth how to play," he said. "Give me the information you have, and Beth will play with you."

A broad smile crossed Madaleine's lips, and challenge gleamed in Nox's eyes.

None of the temper and tension he'd displayed earlier seemed to be present, and I got the impression tonight would be different from my first encounter with the angel of Wrath. She wasn't here to threaten him today, or vice versa. His current enemy was the Ward, not Madaleine, and this was the start of a tentative alliance.

"Deal," she said. "Sloth is running an establishment in Peckham. It's some sort of retreat, with the promise of not having to do anything at all during your stay."

Nox gave a dark chuckle. "That makes sense. Why haven't I heard of it before?"

"I don't believe it's successful enough to be on anyone's radar."

"I suppose that also makes sense. Sloth would hardly make for a decent entrepreneur."

"Cornu." Madaleine snapped her fingers and he appeared over her shoulder, passing her a folded piece of paper. She handed it to Nox. "The address."

"Thank you. I assume this means that you accept the fact that I will not destroy Wrath's page when I recover it?"

Her confident swagger stiffened, and her perfect lips pursed. "I find myself in a position of having to trust you," she said.

"Good. A deal with the devil is binding, I assure you," Nox smiled. His smile sent currents of that delicious confidence surging through me, even though it wasn't aimed at me. He was enjoying this, I realized. He had got one over on her, and his power was rubbing off on me.

"So, how do we play poker?" I asked, buoyed by the feeling.

They both looked at me. Madaleine's tight expression relaxed. "Oh, this should be fun," she beamed.

It turned out that I was not good at poker. I understood the rules quickly enough, and the hierarchy in scoring the cards made intuitive sense to me, but I couldn't bluff. And to make matters worse, Nox kept whispering advice in my ear. He smelled impossibly good, and every time his warm breath moved over my neck, tingles of need shuddered through me and threw off my concentration completely.

"I don't think your friend has it in her to bluff," Madaleine said, holding her cards close to her low cleavage and sipping from her champagne flute.

She was right. I was only going in on hands I knew I would win.

"Do you play cribbage?" I asked hopefully.

Madaleine gave a low laugh. "I'll play anything for money."

"And tonight, you're going to win," Nox said, as I folded yet again.

"Yup." I nodded and finished my drink. "I'm out. No more losing money for me." The chips in front of me weren't mine, Nox had summoned them from yet another well-dressed server, but all the same - I didn't want to pass even more over to Madaleine.

"Very well. Next time, we'll play crib." Her eyes shone, and for the first time, I didn't feel quite as intimidated by her. In fact, I felt a little jealous. She had so much confidence, so much fire, so much sass.

I needed some of that spark for myself. I wanted the feeling Nox gave me to be permanent.

"You're on," I told her.

"Come along, Cornu," she said, standing up and showing off an expanse of creamy skin as the split in her skirt fell open. The demon looked at her as though he wanted to devour her whole and offered her his arm. "I wish you luck with Sloth," Madaleine said to Nox. He gave her a nod of thanks and she left.

"Well. We're going to have to work on your poker skills."

I raised my eyebrows at him. "Why? I don't plan to make a habit of playing."

"No?"

"No. This isn't really my scene."

"You don't like it here?"

"It's not that, exactly. I just don't... fit in."

His hand moved to mine, brushing my fingertips. Sparks of excitement fired through me. "You can fit in anywhere, if that's what you want."

I gave him a look as I shifted on my stool. "You know

as well as I do that's not true. Look at everybody." I gestured around us. "Look at what Madaleine was wearing."

"You would look ten times better in that dress than she did." His voice was low and sultry and his eyes darkened with lust as he spoke.

I wanted to believe him. And his clear desire for me made it a little easier. "Really?"

"Yes. Although, I think you look best with nothing on." He spoke slowly, and my eyes fixed on his sinfully sexy lips as he formed the words. Heat thrummed through my center, pooling at my core.

"Nox," I said, a touch breathlessly. "Stop it."

"Stop what? Trying to arouse you?"

"Yes. You know we can't do anything."

"Not true. We can't have sex."

I froze. "Do you think... we can... do other things?"

"I think we'll only know if we try."

ELEVEN

BETH

Nox took my hand, and stood. I followed him out of the casino, excitement zipping up and down my spine as we went.

I wanted his touch so badly I ached.

He held the car door open for me, and I ducked inside. He climbed in the other side, careful to keep an empty seats worth of space between us, and pressed the button that lowered the electric screen between the cab and the back.

"The long way to Miss Abbott's flat, please Claude."

"Of course, sir."

"And I'd like some music for the journey." Nox looked at me. "Latin?"

I sucked my bottom lip into my mouth as I inhaled. "Latin. Great. Lovely."

A wicked grin took his mouth as Smooth by Santana flowed from the speakers in the car doors.

"Thank you, Claude." At the press of the button, the

screen slid back up. The car was lit only by the night-lights of London through the one-way glass, but the moving lights were plenty enough to see by. "Now, I esti-mate we have thirty minutes until we get to Wimbledon. I want you to stay at yours because I don't think I could have you in my home tonight and not fuck you senseless."

My muscles clenched at his words, heat flooding my chest and neck.

"What about what Adstutus said?"

"I have an idea."

Keeping his eyes fixed on mine, he dropped his hands to his lap. I looked down, and felt my mouth go dry as he unzipped his pants.

The opposite happened between my legs. I felt the hot warmth there as he slowly drew out his erection.

"Nox," I whispered. "What about Claude?"

"Claude can not see or hear us. Undo your trousers."

Command laced his words, and I moved my right hand to the waistband of my own pants.

"Good. Now, we are not going to touch each other. So no power should move from me to you."

I nodded, my cheeks burning.

"We are, however, going to touch ourselves." With his words, he wrapped his fingers around the hard length of his cock.

Once again, I found myself in awe of him, rather than intimidated. He was perfect.

His other hand moved to his shirt, and he began to expertly unbutton it one-handed. "Put you hand in your knickers."

I wanted to. I was desperate for any touch down there, though I'd prefer it was him.

Tentatively, I did as he told me.

His hand moved, up and down. Light flared in his eyes, still locked on mine.

"Tell me."

"Tell you what?" My words were breathy, reflective of my racing pulse.

"Tell me what you feel like."

"Hot. Wet."

He groaned a little, a moved his hand a little faster. The song changed, a powerful drumbeat over sexy Spanish singing. "I wish I was touching you, Beth. I wish it was my fingers. Lift your leg. Move your fingers, as you would want me to."

I dropped my gaze from his face to his lap, and did as he said, lifting one leg up onto the seat and shifting to face him.

This time, I moaned a little.

"Do you like how this looks?" He looked pointedly at his cock.

"Yes."

"Do you have your fingers inside your pussy?"

"Yes."

"Are you imagining me inside you? You on my lap, instead of my hand?"

"Yes."

His hand moved faster, and I matched his pace, doing exactly what he said. I imagined myself in his lap, my legs wrapped around his waist, his hands under my ass and his mouth on my nipples as he bounced me up and down. Filling me.

Heat burst from him, and his hand pumped hard.

"I wish you were fucking me," I whispered, dragging my eyes up to his face.

"Again." His voice was strained, his eyes alive with need.

I moved my own hand faster, my mind filling with every delicious memory of the night we had spent together. I felt my orgasm building, tightening, and had to stop myself moving toward him.

"I wish you were fucking me. I want you so bad."

His hand paused, and I realized he was resisting the urge to move to me too. Then his look sharpened, and his bare chest tensed as he powered his fist up and down himself.

I couldn't help but watch, my own arousal magnified tenfold at the sight of him swelling, stiffening.

"Again," he growled through gritted teeth.

"I wish you were fucking me, hard."

He tensed, stilling for a split second, before letting out a hissing breath as he came over his rock-hard abs.

All the air left my body as I let go, my own stomach and sex convulsing with pleasure as I stared at the beautiful man next to me, waves of release washing over me.

"Fuck, I want you." His eyes bore into mine, intense and heated. "I want to make you come a hundred times harder than that, over and over."

"I want that too."

He moved, grabbing a something from under the seat. Tissues.

I raised my eyebrows at him. "You plan this?"

"Claude keeps a well-stocked car."

We'd barely cleaned up, desperation for him still hammering through me, when he tugged me close.

His fingers stroked down my jaw, and his mouth closed over mine.

His kiss left no question that he felt the same need that I did. Hot as him talking dirty to me whilst stroking himself was, my touch wasn't his.

"We mustn't stay together tonight," He said, as we parted. "I won't be able to resist you." His hand gripped my arm tightly.

I nodded. It was all I could do not to climb into his lap there and then. My aching need for him was returning, pulsing, and I knew he had godlike stamina.

"You know, I've not been able to do that for decades."

"Touch yourself?"

"Yes. It's you, Beth. You're so fucking hot." A shiver of satisfaction went through me, and I kissed him again.

"What if kissing passes power?" I said, the thought making me pull back suddenly.

"I don't think it's kissing that we need to worry about."

"What?"

"Your wings. They lit up. When I came."

Unease replaced the satisfaction fast. "What does that mean?"

"That this isn't an option either." He cupped my

cheek as my face fell. "I think it was worth trying." The warmth in his voice penetrated my worry. "And it can't have done much. Not like spending all night together."

More desire swept through me at the memory of that night. "You're right. It was worth it."

He kissed me, softer this time. "But we can't do it again. It might not be safe."

Claude's voice on the intercom made me jump in surprise. "We're not far from Miss Abbott's, sir."

TWELVE

BETH

I awoke in my own bed the next day, restless and unnerved, and yet again, well before my alarm. It was Thursday, and I decided to use the time I had before work to go and see Francis. She was always up before six.

"Honey, you ain't been here in days, what's happening?" she hollered at me as soon as I walked into the recreation room of Lavender Oaks Retirement home.

"Erm, quite a lot," I said, as I took my usual seat in the tatty wicker chair beside her La-z-boy. "How are you?"

Francis scowled at me. "Orderly says I'm fat. Gotta do me some exercise, or my knee will stop working completely. It's already on its way out."

"I'll exercise with you," I offered immediately. Exercise might help me work off some of my tension.

"Thanks, hon." She patted me knee. "Now. Tell me. Is Mr. Nox as good as he looks like he should be in bed?"

I felt my cheeks heat. "Yes," I said. "Yes he is."

Francis clapped her hands together and beamed at me. "I am so pleased for you! Ain't nothing like good sex to keep a girl's spirits up."

"Well, there's kind of a catch."

Her beam faltered. "Catch?"

"Yeah. When we have sex, a teeny bit of his power gets transferred to me."

Creases formed between her eyebrows as she stared at me. "Devil power?"

"Uhuh."

"Wait, does that mean you're the devil now?"

I barked a laugh. "No. I sure as hell hope not."

"So what does it mean?"

"We're not really sure. We went to see an ancient genie who suggested that it was definitely not a good thing, for him or me."

"You went to see a what now?"

"Genie."

"Huh."

I blew out a sigh and leaned back in the chair. "So now we're trying to lift his curse, because we think that's what's causing the power to get transferred. And also because he got a warning from a god that he would need to be at his full strength because his brothers are plotting against him. But he is worried that when we lift the curse and he gets strong again that he'll be too... *something* for me to like him anymore."

"Something?"

"Devil-like, I suppose," I said with a shrug. I didn't

tell her that just being within a few feet of him when he was mad caused my whole body to kick into fight-or-flight. And I certainly wasn't going to mention what I'd seen him do to Max.

"Are you worried about that?"

I regarded her a moment and then nodded. "Yes. I don't believe that he his evil. He is a keeper of evil, a punisher of evil. And he is dangerous, for sure. But I don't believe he is the *cause* of sin. He gets no pleasure from cruelty. I can feel his soul when we're together..." I trailed off, realizing I sounded a little crazy. "Does that sound stupid?"

"It sounds like you like him. A lot."

"I do. I don't want him to change."

"Maybe he won't. Or he'll change for the better."

I gave her a look. "The man went without sex or food for eight decades because he didn't want to be whatever he was before. I don't think it's going to be better."

"You make a good point," Francis said, and shoved her thumbnail in her mouth thoughtfully.

"Oh, and there's something else."

Francis shifted in her chair to look at me. "I'm listening."

"Alex... Alex was killed. Murdered."

Her jaw fell open slowly, the nail she had gnawing on dropping to her lap. "Aw honey, I'm sorry."

"Yeah. And it was a magical murder, so the magical police are involved, and they think Nox had something to do with it."

"Shit," she said. I nodded. "Did he have something to do with it?"

"No," I said, without hesitation. "He think's it's something to do with wolf shifters."

"Like werewolves?"

"Exactly."

"Well, shit," she repeated. "Who'd have thought werewolves were real."

"My new colleague in the research department is a vampire," I said, suddenly needing to share that information. Francis' eyes lit up.

"Is he hot?"

"No."

Her face fell. "I thought he might me like that man from the film with the big sword. The one that hunts vampires but is a vampire. He's hot."

"Are you talking about Blade?" I asked her.

"I dunno. The guy was hot though."

I shook my head. "I don't even want to know what other films you've been watching."

"I love films. Me and Ethel are watching the second Fifty Shades movie tomorrow. I can't wait."

She rubbed her hands together as I tried to rid my brain of an image of pensioners tied up in the red room. "That'll be nice," I said slowly.

"You know, I think it will."

The train ride into work felt strange. I was starting to become aware that magic people might be able to see the wings on my back, and it was leading me to scrutinize anybody whose gaze lingered on me too long.

Get over yourself, Beth, I told myself. *Nobody cares about your tiny devil wings.*

The devil's power. *In me.*

The thought was still too much to properly digest, even though I'd had a few days now to think about it.

I didn't feel any different.

The small bounces in confidence that I was getting had started before I'd slept with Nox. I had no doubt he was the cause of them, but it felt more like something inside me was being unlocked, something that had always been there. Not like something new had been added.

When I walked into the lobby of LMS the receptionist waved at me, hurrying out from behind his desk. I slowed, anticipation making my nerves tingle.

"Mr. Nox will meet you here," he said, gesturing at one of the plush couches in the waiting area.

"Oh. Okay." I sat down, but didn't have to wait long. Nox strode into view a moment later, and Claude came through the main doors. I hopped up, and saw Nox's gaze focus on something behind me, before settling on my face.

I didn't turn. I knew what he was looking at. Maybe my new awareness of the wings wasn't unfounded after all.

"Good morning," he said.

Just two words, but they fired memories like a confetti gun, images of him with his cock in his hand in the back of the car.

"Hmmpf," I said, and fell into step beside him.

"We are going to visit Sloth. I assumed you would want to accompany me."

I jerked my head up, sex-addled thoughts fleeing instantly. "Sloth? Now?"

"That was the point of the meeting with Madaleine."

And there was my brain, all but deleting everything that had happened before the car ride home.

It took more than half an hour to drive to our destination, and after forty-five minutes of trying to fend off thoughts of jumping the man beside me in broad daylight, I was relieved when he spoke.

"Tell me something about yourself."

I looked at him. He had taken off his suit jacket, as the day was warm, and his top button was undone. He looked relaxed on the leather seat, but his bright eyes were lively, his mouth quirking in that way I'd never seen anyone else's do.

"Like what?"

"Something nobody else knows." Wickedness gleamed in the blue.

"You already know me in a way nobody else does," I said, swallowing my shyness.

"I can't tell you how much I love hearing that," he

half-growled. "But for once, I'm not trying to seduce you." His eyes flicked over my shoulder again, and I resisted the urge to look, too. "I want to know more about you, Beth."

Warmth trickled through me, and it wasn't his power. It was my own ego, swelling at the idea that this man wanted more from me the physical.

"My favorite color is purple," I said, with a small smile.

"That's good, but I was hoping for more."

"I know. I thought I'd start small, and we can work our way up. Your turn." The confidence was going to my head.

"Yellow."

"Yellow? The devil's favorite color is yellow?"

"You were expecting the color of fire and blood?" He raised one eyebrow, and I felt a little guilty. I *had* thought he'd say red. "The fire part is close. I like the yellow you see at the tip of a flame, just before it turns white."

His accent was heavy, and he was speaking slowly, and I found myself watching his lips, my own parting. God, I'd never known the power of speech over my libido before meeting him. I could get off on his voice alone.

"That's a nice color," I mumbled when I realized he was waiting for me to respond.

"What kind of books do you like to read?" He asked me, the smile playing across his lips making it clear that he knew what I was thinking about.

I cleared my throat. "How do you know I like to read?"

"I've been in your apartment. There were books everywhere."

I narrowed my eyes at him, then shrugged. "Romance. I like romance books."

"Romance books with sex in them?"

"I thought this wasn't about sex."

He nodded at me. "You're right. It's not."

"Do you read?" I remembered that he'd had loaded bookshelves in his study, but that thought led to the memory of me being bent over his couch, his expert tongue-

"Yes. I read."

My face was aflame now. "What do you read?"

"Everything."

"Romances with sex in them?" I asked before I could stop myself.

"Yes. But I thought we weren't talking about sex?"

"It's hot. In the car." *Pull yourself together, Beth.*

Nox pressed a button on the door panel beside him, and cool air began to blow over me from nowhere.

"Better?"

The smile on his face told me he knew why I was hot. But I wasn't going to give him the satisfaction of acknowledging it. "Much. Thank you. What do you like to read the most?"

He paused, then answered, "Historical fiction."

"Oh yeah?"

"Yes. I have been around a long time, and I like to see the different fantasies of what could have been. The fictional stories of those I could have passed on the street."

"That's sort of what I like too. Someone on the train next to me could be living the story I'm reading, for all I know."

"Did you ever imagine that they might have wings? Or turn into a lion?" he smiled.

"Actually, yes. I've never had trouble imagining magic around me. And when I lost my parents, I couldn't believe that they could vanish, so I let myself believe a little more."

Nox moved his hand slowly, wrapping his fingers around mine. "You were right. You should have trusted your instincts."

"Well, until I met you, it wouldn't have made any difference anyway. Believing in the Veil doesn't allow you to see behind it. Right?"

"Right," he nodded. "I'm sorry we are not looking for your parents now. But we will." His hand squeezed mine, and an unexpected bubble of emotion rose inside me. I had never, ever had help looking for them. It was something I had done alone, obsessed over alone.

Given up on alone.

"I understand. And I'm grateful."

"It is extremely unlikely that they are in danger, or we would have begun the search already. If they were lost years ago, then..." His eyes grew dark, and tension took his face.

I knew what he was trying to find the words to say. "Then they are already dead," I finished for him.

His grip tightened.

"It's okay. I know that it's the most likely outcome," I told him. "I have already mourned their loss, and I'm not going to go through that again if I can help it. I just can't stand the thought of not knowing. And if there's even a glimmer of hope that something else happened, that they are living a life hidden from me..." I didn't know why they would abandon me. We had been close; my father and I, especially. It seemed unlikely that they packed up one day to go and hide themselves in magic. Impossible, even.

But the fact remained, I didn't know. And I needed to.

"I'm sorry."

"For what?"

"That this happened to you."

His words were loaded with sincerity, and the bubble of emotion in my gut swelled. He moved his head an inch, as though he wanted to kiss me, but thought better of it.

I closed the distance, and when our lips met it was completely new. It wasn't the heated, hungry sharing of passion our previous embraces had been. It was deeper, softer. So *real*.

His hand moved to cup my cheek, as gently as his tongue found mine.

He cared. He cared about me.

I could feel his power, his energy, his presence wrapping around me like armor. He was trying to protect me, and the threat was my own sadness.

I kissed him harder, overwhelmed suddenly at having someone to share the burden with. His touch on my cheek spread, his fingers splaying, pulling my face tighter to his.

After a blissful moment, his lips left mine, but by no more than an inch. He gazed into my eyes, blue flames dancing in his irises. "Your strength is beautiful."

"What?" I breathed.

"Your strength. Your determination. Your hope. You're glorious."

If the moment had been less intimate I would have laughed. "*My* strength?"

"There is fire inside you, Beth. But you don't wield it as I am used to. It's..." He drew in breath. "I want more."

I blinked. He leaned in, kissing me softly once more, before letting me go.

"I... I wish I could see myself as you see me," I whispered. There was something that really could have been adoration in his face, and I couldn't make sense of it. I was literally the most boring person I knew. Or had been, until I met Nox.

"So do I. I will make it my undying mission to never rest until you see yourself as I do." His words were hard, like ringing steel, and they caused a surge of that delicious confidence to course through me like a shot to the veins. "And if I have to do it without laying a finger on you, I will."

THIRTEEN

BETH

The warm, fuzzy feeling Nox had planted squarely in my gut wavered when we got out of the car a few short minutes later.

The building in front of us had the potential to be quite nice. It was part of a row of tall townhouse buildings, but it stood out because it had Greek style columns either side of the door, and a large plaque reading Sacred Sleep Spa.

I stopped as Nox went to push open the door. "This place doesn't feel right," I said. "It's like all the good stuff you just made me feel is leaving me."

Something strained flickered through Nox's eyes when he turned to me. "Sloth was always my least favorite sin," he said darkly. "People think Sloth is just laziness. It's not. It is the disinclination to act when you could help. It can lead to the loss or ruination of someone's life just as easily as wrath or greed, but it utterly lacks the passion that drive the others. I am not saying that I condone sins driven by passion," he said, holding his hand up. "But I can assure you, many of the worst punishments I have doled out have been to those who don't even have the energy to care. They feel no remorse, they don't see any responsibility for themselves or anyone around them. It is an appalling way to live."

He spoke with such disgust, it bordered on anger. And now, he had to try to get this sin he hated back. I wished I could say something helpful to him, but I had nothing to offer. Sloth had sounded much worse than just not bothering to do the dishes when he described it like that.

"You will feel all your drive and enthusiasm leaving you if he isn't controlling his power properly. Madaleine keeps fairly tight control of hers, because she has to; Wrath is explosive. But it looks like Sloth may be using his power differently."

He glanced up at the day spa sign distastefully, then back to me. "Would you like to wait in the car?"

"No." I wasn't going to hide in the car from the angel of doing-fuck-all.

I regretted my decision the moment we walked through the doors.

The smell hit me first.

Stagnant water, mixed with rotting food. I felt the back of my throat close up. As much of me that didn't want to breathe through my nose didn't want to open my mouth, either.

We were in a tiled reception area, and the woman behind the desk stared at us without speaking.

The tiles might once have been cream, but they were now so grimy it was hard to tell. Water stains covered the painted walls, and there was litter everywhere—empty chip-bags and candy wrappers. Rusted pipes ran the height of the room, making unnerving burping and clanking sounds.

"I'm here to see your boss," Nox said to the woman.

She shrugged her shoulders, the threadbare fabric of her shirt falling down with the motion, exposing her too-thin collarbone and shoulder. Her hair was filthy, her gray eyes sunken.

Nox looked at her a second longer and then headed toward the only other door in the room.

The reception was positively pleasant compared to the room beyond.

Warm, stuffy heat rolled over us, and the smell intensified with it. I lifted my arm to my face, burying my nose in the crook of my elbow and trying to inhale the smell of washing powder.

There was a large round pool in the middle of a cavernous room, surrounded by loungers. I could just about see how this might once have been quite a nice spa, but now...

The water was a green-gray color, and moved like sludge rather than liquid. There was trash everywhere I looked, in dark puddles on the tiles that I didn't even want to think about.

There were people on the loungers, some excruciatingly thin, and others so large they didn't fit. None of them were moving.

The room was round, and I could see three doors off it and a large, open archway leading to what looked like another pool at the far end.

"He's this way." Nox started toward the door on the left, and I stepped carefully after him. We passed close to a man on a lounger, and the smell changed, to something distinctly like human excrement. I tightened my arm around my face, trying to breathe through my shirt and not throw up. The man's skin was a sallow yellow color, and I couldn't see his chest moving.

"Is he alive?" I half-hissed to Nox.

He threw a glance at the guy, then me, and kept moving without a word.

I felt sicker.

I had never been somewhere so unpleasant. It was like something out of a horror film.

Nox pushed open the door too hard when we reached it, and it creaked as it swung open, then banged off the wall.

"Sloth?" he barked.

A man looked up from a large armchair, a vacant expression on his face.

An overwhelming urge to lay down took me. *I mean, what was the point of doing much else, really?*

Heat swamped me before my knees could bend,

knocking out the sleepy feeling. A smell of smoke and whiskey accompanied it. It wasn't the humid, disgusting heat of the spa. It was Nox.

A rat ran past my feet, scuttling toward the man in the chair. I suppressed a yelp and stepped closer to Nox. There was nothing else in the large room. Nothing hanging on the wall, no other furniture. Just the guy, alone in a chair.

He was as dirty as the woman on reception, shirtless and pale. Huge red sores covered his skin, and a slow smile crept over his face.

It was creepy as hell.

"The big man," he beamed at Nox.

"What the fuck do you think you're doing?" snarled Nox. "You vowed to control your power, not let people fucking die under it!"

Shit, did that mean that guy out there *was* dead? More nausea rolled through me.

"It's hard, man. It's hard. I mean, shit, you know it's hard. You did it before me." The lazy smile was still plastered on his face, his brown eyes vacant.

"Where's the page?" Nox hissed.

"Dunno. I used to have it. But it's gone now."

Heat crashed over me, and Nox's wings appeared, unfurling. It was utterly wrong to see something so beautiful in a place so foul.

"How long ago did you lose it?" I asked quickly, through my elbow.

"Like, maybe..." he looked thoughtful. Slowly, his eyes closed.

"Sloth!" Nox roared. He jerked awake.

"A week ago?" Sloth said.

That recent? I looked at Nox. "Was it stolen?"

"Yeah, man."

Nox cursed. "You're a fucking disgrace," he growled.

A slow chuckle left Sloth, which rapidly turned into a cough. "Yeah," he said, when he got his breath back. "I heal every night. Then each morning, this. Fucking disgraceful." He laughed again.

"Nox, can we go?" I wasn't sure I could control my gag reflex much longer.

"Yes. But heed me, Sloth. I will be back, and you will pay for your negligence."

"Put me out of my fucking misery, man," Sloth grinned at him. "I'm done."

I leaned against the wall when we got outside, the petrol fumes of the London air tasting as sweet as honey compared to whatever we'd been breathing in the spa.

"I need a bath. I need every bit of that place off me, now," I breathed.

"My place is closer than yours." Fury still rolled from him in waves.

"No sex," I said. I knew going to his was a bad idea, especially to be naked and wet, but I hadn't been exaggerating. I needed the stench of that place gone from me, or my breakfast would make a reappearance.

"No sex. Your own room and bathroom."

"Let's go."

. . .

Beelzebub came crashing toward us as we entered Nox's place, but pulled up at the last minute, nose twitching as he sniffed at us.

"I told you! I told you we stink!" I rubbed at my arms as though they were covered in grime, feeling more unwell than I had in years.

Nox led me straight up the grand staircase, to the same guest room I had stayed in before. "There are some clothes in the wardrobe," he said, gesturing to the closet.

"Your clothes?"

"No. Clothes for you."

We stared at each other a beat. "Why do you have clothes for me here?"

He gave a casual shrug. "Accidents happen. Things catch fire. You know."

I thought of him removing his underwear by burning it to ash, and swallowed. "Right. Forward planning."

"Yes. Spontaneous adventures might be undertaken. Clothes could get torn off. I thought I should be prepared."

God, I wished he could tear my clothes off.

"Well you can incinerate these all you like," I said gesturing at my outfit. "They're covered in death-spa smell. He stepped forward, and I jerked back, throwing my hands up. "I was joking!"

A smile pulled at his mouth. "I know. I'll have them washed." I opened my mouth, but he cut me off. "Thoroughly."

"Fine. Thank you."

He kept staring at me. "You're going to have to give them to me if you want them washed," he said, when I just stared back.

"I'm not getting naked in front of you."

His eyes narrowed, and his shoulders stiffened. "You're probably right."

"I'm definitely right. Go away. I have death-spa on me." Plus, if he stayed much longer I would drag him into the shower with me. The desire in his eyes, the tension in his body, the knowledge of what he could do to me, how he could make me feel-

"Leave! You need to leave!" I pushed at his solid arms, and he responded with sinful smile that made my insides liquify.

"Fine. I'm going. Leave your clothes outside the door."

He took his time leaving the room, and as soon as he was gone I stripped out of my shirt and jeans. I opened the door a crack, flung them out, and raced to the massive shower.

Nox's shower was heaven. It was roughly one million times better than my own shower. The scent of expensive soap gradually replaced the rotten sewage smell that had lodged in my nostrils, and the powerful hot water did its job, removing the lingering feeling of decay.

I wasn't sure how long I'd spent in there, but when I wrapped myself in a towel and stepped out of the bathroom, I felt a whole lot better. Well, cleaner. I still felt horny as hell, but I doubted that was going away any time soon.

I opened the closet and smiled at the selection of clothes. A few pairs of jeans, in blue and black, and a series of pastel colored shirts and scoop-neck Ts. Exactly what I liked to wear. One of the tops was black, and I took out the hanger to look closer. It was an off-shoulder sweater with beautiful diamanté roses across the front.

Pulling open the top drawer in the shelving unit under the rail, I found underwear. Lacy underwear, in both red and black. I bit down on my lip as I lifted a black set up. It felt soft and sensual in my hands, as though the fabric had been invented purely to be a part of something intimate.

That feeling only increased when I pulled on the panties and fastened the bra. So, this was what luxury felt like.

I went with blue jeans and the pretty black sweater, and fished out some mascara and eyeliner from my purse. When I was done, I felt pretty good, but the image of the sallow, bloated guy on the lounger still lingered at the back of my mind.

As I left my room and made my way to the stairs, I wondered on Sloth's words. He didn't want the power anymore. He'd told Nox he was done. And I could understand why. What a freaking awful way to live. It was so at odds with Nox's vibrant, fiery energy. I couldn't imagine him wanting that sort of power anywhere near him, or what it must have been like to try to control it.

"Hi," I said, walking into the kitchen that I loved even

more than the shower. Bright light streamed over the countertops from the roof light, and Beelzebub stormed toward me, claws clattering.

I dropped to my knees before he could bowl me over, and he rolled onto his back so I could scratch his belly, tongue lolling out to the side.

"How was your shower?" Nox asked. He was sitting on a stool, shirt-sleeves rolled up. His hair was damp. He must have showered too. The thought of him naked crashed into my mind, standing under the running water, hard and ready, those sinfully wicked eyes boring into mine...

"Good. Thank you," I said, dragging my eyes from his beautiful face and focusing on the dog. "But I have a bunch of questions for you."

"Of course you do. You always do."

FOURTEEN

BETH

"I thought that it might be easier to resist temptation," -I squirmed as he said the word *temptation* unnecessarily slowly-, "if we went out."

"Oh. Okay, sure." I gave the dog a last scratch and stood up. "Where?"

"Well, it's too early for dinner..." He cocked his head at me thoughtfully. His hair moved, falling down the side of his face, and I barely resisted the urge to step forward and run my fingers through it. He drew in a slow breath, as though he'd sensed my urge too. "Come on."

Before I could do or say anything else, he marched past me, toward the front of the house. I trotted after him, surprised to see a pair of black ankle boots by the front door.

"Are they for me?"

"Yes. Unless you would prefer something different?"

I crouched down to look at them as he slid his own feet into immaculate, expensive looking loafers. The boots I was holding were equally as nice, I realized. "No, they're great, but..." I looked up at him. "It feels weird, you buying me expensive stuff. Without me knowing."

He raised one eyebrow. "Beth, I don't know how well you recall the conversations we have had since meeting one another, but I have never been more interested in a human as I am in you. I knew before you spent the night here that I would want you in my home as much as was physically possible. And, as I already told you, I have a habit of setting fire to fabric." He wet his lips as he stared down at me, and I became distinctly aware of my submissive position. I didn't stand up though.

"Having now spent the night with you, I am quite certain that I made the right decision. And the things I have bought are expensive because I like expensive things, and I can't keep them for myself."

"You can't keep them for yourself?" I asked, choosing not to respond to anything else he had said.

"No. Not if they are overly expensive. Just like my money, it all goes overnight, unless I give it away."

"So, what about those shoes?"

"Bought new for me today."

My mouth dropped open. "Seriously? You buy new shoes everyday?"

"Yes. And suits, or watches, some days. Rory keeps both my home and office stocked with clothes and such daily."

"That's insane," I said.

"It's how it is. They used to vanish overnight. Now, I make sure they go to good homes instead."

"The devil is into charity?"

"The devil isn't the asshole everyone thinks he is," Nox rumbled. "The devil is supposed to punish the assholes."

I nodded as I straightened, and pulled on the boots. They fit perfectly, soft material moulding to my feet like magic. "Well, if you're not a part of the assholery, thank you for the lovely boots," I said.

He laughed, a loud, real laugh that made my chest swell and a smile stretch across my face. "I like that. Assholery," he repeated in his Irish accent.

I grinned at him, and he swept an arm out suddenly, drawing me to him and kissing me. It was over too fast, but he was smiling as he drew back. "Let's go on a date, Miss Abbott."

"What do you think?"

"I freaking love aquariums!" I was aware that I sounded like a small, over-excited child as I beamed at him, and I didn't care. It was true. Nox had brought me to the London Aquarium, and I was practically bouncing on the balls of my feet as he handed me my ticket.

His eyes were dancing with light as he watched me. "If we wait half an hour, we can have the place to ourselves."

"What? Don't be silly. We don't need the place to ourselves to look at fish!" I grabbed his hand and tugged him toward the turnstiles.

"But, there are so many people," he said, looking around himself. "And children."

I laughed. "You're taller than the kids. You can look over their heads," I told him. He scowled at me, but let me lead him to the entrance.

"You know," he said as he fed his ticket into the machine and the bar lifted. "I usually have private entrances to things. It has been a long time since I used one of these contraptions."

I rolled my eyes as I moved through the one next to him. "Then it's about time you reminded yourself what it's like to be one of the peasants."

He grunted.

The aquarium was hot and dark and humid, but in an exciting way, totally different to the cesspit of a spa we had visited earlier. The vivid blues everywhere lifted my spirits, and I tugged Nox from one room to another, trying to spot sharks and rays and hidden creatures in the enormous tanks, and reading excitedly to him from the information boards about the animals that had been rescued and housed.

He said little, and the only things he watched with as much interest as he watched me were the slow movements of the bigger, predatory creatures.

A shark glided past us as we stepped into a tunnel through the largest tank, shoals of bright fish fluttering over the top of us.

"Aren't they awesome?" I breathed, speeding my

pace to try to keep up with it. Tough gray skin, razor sharp teeth, dark beady eyes... I found sharks both beautiful and terrifying.

The connection with the man beside me settled in my brain, and I glanced at him.

"Yes. Deadly, and graceful." His eyes were fixed on me, not the shark. "I'm pleased you find a predator like that appealing."

I swallowed nervously, images of Max screaming flashing into my mind. "Sharks are part of the food chain, a whole ecosystem. They are built to survive," I said.

Nox nodded. "They do not kill for sport."

"No."

I wasn't completely sure what we were saying to each other, and when a boy of about six streaked past us yelling "Look!" I was relieved the moment was broken.

"The map said there were coral fish in the next room. Let's go."

We spent about an hour in the aquarium, and I was buzzing with energy when we emerged into the early evening light. We were between the huge London Eye and Westminster Bridge, prime tourist spots for good reason. Big Ben towered over the Houses of Parliament on the other side of the river, looking magnificent.

"Are you ready for dinner?" Nox asked me.

"Yes," I nodded enthusiastically.

"We need to go over the bridge."

He took my hand, and we walked together along the river, until we reached the bridge.

"You said you had questions for me, earlier."

"I did, and then you distracted me with sea-life."

He smiled as we started over the river. "I have organized some privacy for us for our meal, so you can ask me anything you like then."

"Okay. Where are we eating?" I could feel myself giving up on being uncomfortable about the amount of money Nox spent, especially knowing he couldn't take it into the next day. Why not give it to the chefs and servers in nice restaurants?

"There." Nox pointed, and I frowned as I realized he was pointing to the water. I peered over the columns edging the bridge, and saw a squat, glass-sided boat docked at the pier.

"We're eating on the boat?"

"Yes."

"Will it be moving?" I couldn't keep the excitement from my voice. I'd wanted to do a River Thames tour since moving to the city.

Nox chuckled. "Yes. It will take us to Tower Bridge, then back."

I squeezed his hand and beamed at him. "I can't wait."

FIFTEEN

BETH

The boat was dressed beautifully, as nice as any restaurant I had seen. A smiling man had greeted us as we had made our way down the pier, and offered to help me across the small gangplank onto the boat - until Nox had glared at him and offered me his own hand. A feeling that I had never got from being with Alex filled me at the possessive gesture.

The boat interior was pretty much all one room, with toilets at the back and a bar against the front wall and doors that I assumed led to the kitchen. Two tables had been set against each of the glass sides, and they wouldn't have looked out of place at a wedding reception.

"Wow," I said. "This is amazing."

"The view is best on the right, but if you would prefer to sit on the left that is no problem," smiled our host.

I waited for Nox to answer for us, but he just looked at me. "Oh. We'll take your advice, right is great," I said.

Once we were seated, he came back with menus, and it didn't take me long to choose my meal.

"We're on a boat, so I think it's appropriate I have fish," I told Nox, having ordered the seabass.

He cocked his head. "I fancy something... meatier," he said.

Before I could say anything, I felt movement, and whipped my head to the window. We were off, moving at a gentle pace along the river Thames.

"This is awesome," I said. "Thank you."

"You're welcome. I wanted to offset the unpleasantness of this afternoon. Give you something more cheerful to remember about today."

"I'm grateful," I said, as we passed the aquarium we had just come from.

The host brought over a bottle of wine, and I realized it was something sparkling when it popped on opening.

"This is a different way to spend a Thursday evening," I said, lifting the champagne flute once it was full and we were alone again.

"Well, you had better get used to it."

I bit my lip. "I guess if I carry on spending this much time with you, I'll have to get used to the other stuff too."

His face darkened. "What other stuff are you referring to?"

"All of it," I shrugged. "I'm excited to get used to magic, and my new job, and to some extent the unknown but... Dead bodies on loungers is a lot."

"I didn't realize Sloth had let control get so far from him," Nox said, voice tight. "I would have gone alone."

"That's not the point. I don't want to be protected from everything. If I'm going to be with you, if we're going to find your sins and the book and my parents, then I guess I'm going to have to toughen up. I guess the champagne comes with corpses."

A look I'd seen a few times fired in his eyes, and I thought it was respect, or admiration. "I told you that you were strong."

"I'm trying to believe you."

He lifted his glass. "To your strength," he said.

"To champagne and corpses," I replied.

"What's Sloth's real name?"

"George Simmons."

I took another bite of delicious seabass before continuing. "And was he telling you that he didn't want the power any more?"

I knew that was what he had said, but I wanted Nox to confirm it.

"Yes. My memory of that accursed power is clearly correct. I hated carrying it. I hated seeing it in people. I hated what it made people do, what it made people *allow*." Shadows swept across his irises.

"If you take the power back, will you..." I tried to think of a way to word my question, but Nox gave me a small smile over his steak.

"End up like him? No."

"Why not?"

"I am immeasurably stronger than him, for one, and my other powers will override Sloth."

"Even if you don't have all the others back yet?"

"Yes. My existing powers are enough. Lust and Greed are particularly powerful."

"Do you use your powers on people?" I wasn't sure if I wanted the answer, and I already knew that his Lust magic affected me.

"I did, for a while, when I first gave up the other sins. But I did not enjoy the consequences."

I looked at him in question, and he gave me a long look before carrying on.

"I had spent an eternity punishing those who abused the sins, and I wanted to see where human limits were. I wanted to see where Greed tipped from fun to lethal. Where Gluttony moved from enjoyable to painful. I knew the power of the sins, and I couldn't believe that they were all evil. Particularly the three I kept. I knew what Sloth did to people so there was no curiosity for me there, and Wrath has no questions around it - anger makes people violent. Pride bored me, and Envy would have been too easy to abuse. So, I tested people."

"Is that when the Ward fell out with you?" I asked the question as mildly as I could.

"Yes."

"Did you...do anything really bad?"

"Nothing worse than I did under the orders of gods." True darkness filled his eyes when he spoke this time, and I hurried to change the subject.

"Do you think Sloth's page was taken by the same people who paid Max to steal your book?"

"I think that it is not good if that is the case. I don't know what they think they can do with the books and the pages without me, but they would be unlikely to be doing this with no reason. There must be some plan."

"I can't believe it was stolen so recently." My frustration came out in my tone. "We were so close."

"It is highly unfortunate."

A loud thump from above us made us both look sharply upward. A scratching, scrabbling sound followed.

"What's that?" Before I finished the question, Nox was standing, his chair flying backward. His golden wings snapped out behind him, filling the space and taking my breath away.

"Get behind me, now," he said and his voice was laced with lethal menace. I pushed my own chair back, dropped my knife and fork, then hurried toward him.

"What's happening?"

"Hellhounds," he hissed.

There were more scrabbling noises, and a cry from somewhere outside the room. "What?" I failed to keep the panic from my voice.

"Large, dangerous dogs from my realm. They should not be here in London. Get behind me, now."

Dark shadows swept across his gleaming gold feathers as I moved wide to get around his wings and do as he asked.

An almighty crash made my hands fly to my ears, then light streamed in from above us as something crashed through the ceiling. The dark mass landed with a whacking thud just a foot from where I stood.

Shaking itself, a giant hound straightened up, onto all fours. My heart skipped a beat as it locked its bright scarlet eyes on mine.

Holy hell.

The thing looked like a doberman had been doubled in size and weight, and had flames added to its fur. Actual fire licked up and down its sleek, inky coat, and saliva dripped from its snout as it bared razor-edged teeth at me and snarled.

"Nox," I whispered, surprised any sound came out at all. The thing's head was as high as mine, and literally inches away. I could smell the meaty stench of its breath.

Heat smashed over me, and my knees buckled under a force that wasn't natural. I was aware of something bright and hot moving over my head as I crashed to the ground, rolling in the direction I knew Nox was in. The dog lunged forward too, under whatever had been hurled at it. For a terrifying instant, its snout met my shoulder, but glanced off. I got a fleeting glimpse of a symbol, tattooed inside its massive ear, as I rolled, and then it yelped in pain and vanished from my churning view.

When I came to a stop I scrambled to my knees, trying to get my bearings. Nox's golden wings were wrapped around him and the hellhound, fire billowing from the dog and engulfing him.

Fear for Nox gripped me, and a strangled sound

came from my throat. Then there was a growl that I was sure came from Nox, not the dog, and a shadow as dark as an abyss swelled before him. The hound shrieked and turned, leaping for the hole he'd made in the roof of the boat. The shadow moved with him, though, dragging him back down. Nox raised both hands, his wings extending wide, and a pure, unadulterated terror took me in its hold.

I knew the feeling. It was the same as when I'd been on the quayside with Rory, when Nox had punished Max.

But something was different this time. Something deep inside me was responding, but not with fear. *With heat.* The overwhelming need to scream and cry and hide was being met with a contradiction, a surge of defiance.

With something just as dark as what I was so terrified of.

Nox roared, and the shadow folded in on itself, taking the hellhound with it, both of them vanishing with a loud crack. An awful, animal sound of pain echoed around the space, and then everything around me fell silent, my heaving breaths the only thing audible.

A scraping sound cut through the stillness, and we both whirled to see the boat host standing at the other end of the room, his face as white as a sheet. He took one look at Nox and fainted.

Nox moved toward me fast, wrapping an arm around my waist. I tried to speak, but a pointless croak came out. His shirt and a large chunk of his trousers had burned away.

"We're going home," he said into my ear, before pressing me tighter to his side, and beating his wings.

I barely had time to catch my breath before we were soaring through the hole in the boat. He beat his wings harder and cold air streamed over me, my eyes blurring fast and obscuring the view of Nox's incredible wings, and London beyond them.

My already adrenaline-overloaded system must have decided this was too much, because rather than be scared to death, a weird calm took hold of me, my shaking limbs settling and my queasy stomach falling still. I wrapped my arms tight around his neck, trying to focus on his epic wings, knowing with utter certainty that his grip around my middle wouldn't waver.

I felt like I was in a dream, a dazed detachment refusing to let me acknowledge we were flying.

Instead, one thought was churning through my skull.

Was it Nox's power—the darkness inside me—that had stood up to the fear?

SIXTEEN

BETH

We landed on the roof terrace of Nox's house, right beside the pool. I focused on it as he gently set me down, my feet throbbing weirdly as they touched the tiles.

"Are you alright?" He loosened his grip around my waist slowly, then held my face in his hands, pulling my gaze up to his. "Beth, are you alright?" he repeated.

"I felt it," I said.

He frowned. "The hellhound? Did it hurt you?"

"No. No, I felt the power. Your power."

He stiffened, something sparking in his eyes. "What do you mean?"

"When you did your scary bastard thing, something tried to fight the fear. Something just as scary and dark. Inside me."

Nox stared at me, and I stared back. "You're pale," he said eventually. "Let's get inside."

I nodded. I still felt detached from reality. I let him lead me downstairs, instead of to the bedrooms.

He took me to the study we'd been in before, which was soft and warm and dark, and full of books. He sat me down on the couch, and I was still dazed enough that only a fleeting memory of the last time I'd been on the couch slipped into my head.

"Nox, do I have devil power?"

He let out a long breath. "Give me a few minutes to change," he said. I realized his wings were still visible, tucked tight to his back. "Then we'll talk."

He returned dressed in jeans and a t-shirt, something I had never seen him wear. He passed me one of two tumblers half-filled with amber liquid.

"For the shock," he said, and sat down next to me. "You do have some of my power inside you, but it does not mean you are dark or evil," he said, before I could speak. There were no shadows in his eyes, there was no playful quirk to his lips. Just sincerity in those bright blue orbs. "If the only thing that has triggered any of that power is a need to defend yourself against more of it, I would say that is a good thing." He took a sip of his whiskey, and I wondered why. He couldn't taste it. It reminded me that I could taste mine, though, so I took a small sip. It burned all the way down my throat, and my thoughts cleared a little. I repeated what he had just said, in my head.

He was right. If it could only be triggered by him, and it was trying to defend me, that was good.

"Why did a hellhound attack us?"

His jaw tightened, but still no telltale signs of anger showed. "One of two reasons. Someone inside my realm is working against me and let it loose."

"And the other?" I prompted when he stopped speaking.

He swallowed. "My power has weakened sufficiently that I can't keep the hellhounds contained from here in London."

"Shit," I mumbled. "They both sound pretty bad."

"If we hear more reports of loose hellhounds, it's likely the latter."

"I saw a tattoo," I remembered. "Inside its ear."

Nox's eyebrows drew together. "Hellhounds are feral. They would not have tattoos."

"Well, this one did. It was of a bell."

"A bell? When you are next at work, please talk to Malcolm about this, and begin researching. It could be important."

I nodded. We fell quiet, each sipping our drinks without speaking. "I, erm, would like to do that again sometime," I said eventually.

"Fight a hellhound?" Nox stared at me in disbelief.

"No! Fly," I corrected him quickly. "There is no fucking way I want to fight a hellhound again."

A smile pulled at his mouth. "I like it when you swear."

"Huh."

His face turned serious again. "I'm sorry. Both that my power scared you, and that the first time I flew with you wasn't different."

"Let's pretend it didn't happen," I said. "The flying, I mean. Your power scaring me is another thing I think I'm going to have to get used to."

"I was created to punish. And for punishment to be effective, the receiver must fear it. Terror is as much a part of my power as the rest of my magic."

He didn't speak with apology in his tone, but there was a strain to his matter-of-factness.

"I understand," I said. And I sort of did. But it didn't make it any easier. The man who cupped my cheek and filled my core with need was so at odds with the shadowy monster he kept contained inside him. Even his wings didn't match the darkness, gleaming and golden as they were.

"Are you feeling better?" he asked me.

"Yes. Tired now, actually."

"That'll be the adrenaline wearing off. You should stay here tonight."

I didn't argue. I knew how comfortable his beds were, both his own and the guest room. And I had no desire to head back out into the night. Or be alone.

"Could a hellhound have ripped out Alex's throat?" I asked, the thought tumbling from my mouth at the same time it occurred to me. The memory of those saliva-covered fangs made me gulp down more warming whiskey.

"Perhaps. It would explain the strong magic signature. Mention that to Malcolm too."

"Okay."

"I knew you would be good at this new job." He smiled at me, and a little flurry of confidence bubbled through me.

"Detective Abbott, at your service." I gave him a tired smile. Fatigue was building quickly, now that I'd admitted to it.

"Come on." He stood up and held out his hand, and I took it.

I was tired enough that I only felt a pang of disappointment to be led to the guest room that I had showered in earlier, instead of Nox's room.

SEVENTEEN

NOX

I glared down at my drink. Fuck, I wished I could taste it.

Knowing Beth was upstairs was a sweet kind of torture. I had promised her she would see herself as I saw her. Strong and fierce, but with no pride or wrath. Just honest determination and soul.

But I couldn't do it through the power of intimacy.

I knew a part of me had made that promise because I feared I would let her down. When it came to making a choice between being with her and my freedom, I still didn't know what I would do. But I would find a way to make her happy, regardless.

I ground my teeth as I tried to clear my thoughts.

If hellhounds were loose, then I needed to visit hell. And if I visited hell, then I could not avoid Examinus. If I were in his presence, then he would know that my power was waning.

I gripped the glass too hard, and it shattered, the

amber liquid spilling over my hand.

Beth had felt my power, responding to me. What did that mean?

My phone rang, and I got an unpleasant tingle down my spine. I stiffened. I knew what that meant.

The screen of my cell said 'Private Number' but I knew it was one of two men on the other end.

"What?" I growled as I answered.

"Is that any way to greet a brother?" It was Michael. The slightly more obnoxious of my two angel siblings.

"What do you want?"

"I've heard that things aren't going particularly well for you just now."

"You heard wrong."

"Oh, I don't think so. Rumor has it that you've lost the Book of Sins."

"I will recover it," I spat.

"And that you're a suspect in a murder."

"I had nothing to do with it." I instantly regretted taking his bait. I could hear the smile in his voice as he replied.

"Let's meet. Gabriel wants to be a part of this too."

"A part of what? I hear my own rumors, you know."

"Oh yes?"

"Yes. And my sources are stronger than yours." I emphasized the word stronger, and Michael gave a chuckle.

"Examinus been on about his imaginary war again, has he? I assure you, brother, we have no part in anything the gods are getting up to."

I didn't trust him any more than I trusted Examinus. "Why do you want to meet?"

"A number of reasons. I'll make it worth your while. I have information about the murder that the Ward are trying to keep under wraps from you specifically."

Anger kindled in my gut. "Are you trying to bribe me? What do you want?"

"We want to help you."

"Help me?"

"Recover your power."

I frowned. "Why?"

"Meet with us. We will discuss it properly in person, not over this silly electronic contraption."

Michael knew he had won, I could hear it in his voice. I couldn't *not* find out what he knew. More information was always better than less. But it would be on my terms.

"My casino, Provoco. Saturday night, ten."

"Fine. Oh, and please, bring your new human friend. I've heard a lot about her."

Before I could speak, he hung up. I snarled at the phone.

I couldn't begrudge him being well-informed. I kept myself well-informed for the same reasons. And anybody with any interest in me would have noticed Beth by now. There was no point trying to keep her away from them.

But would they see my power in her? That could give them an edge I did not want them to have over her or me. It was Thursday. I had two days to find a way to hide her wings before she met my brothers.

EIGHTEEN

BETH

"There," I said, finishing my small sketch and holding it up to the camera for Malc. "That's what the symbol in the dogs ear looked like." The vampire frowned down the lens at it.

"I've never seen it before. Take a photo and email it to me, I'll try some reverse image searches."

"Okay."

"So," Malc said as I got my cell out to photograph the drawing. "You had an interesting evening last night?"

"You mean the hellhound?"

"Erm, yeah? What the fuck else would I mean?"

I gave him a look. "The devil took me on a date to the aquarium. That's quite interesting too."

"I guess you're right."

"Do vampires date?" I asked him, cocking my head.

"Not in a longterm capacity," he answered vaguely. "So, what did it look like?"

"What?"

He rolled his eyes at me. "The hellhound. Jeez, are you feeling okay?"

"Tired, actually," I said. And I was. My dreams had been filled with blood and darkness, but I couldn't remember anything more than unsettling impressions each time they woke me.

"Oh. Well, we can talk about it later if you like."

"No, no, it's okay." I described the monstrous dog to him.

"Sounds messed up," he said, eyes gleeful.

"I'm guessing you've never seen one?"

"Beth, nobody's ever seen one. They live in hell."

He spoke like I was an idiot, and I scowled at him. "There's other weird stuff here in London," I protested. "How was I supposed to know hellhounds don't visit?"

He raised his eyebrows at me. "Do me a favor. If you see a giant flaming beast on the London Underground, do not assume it is supposed to be there," he said, shaking his head. "Run."

"Right. Thanks for the tip." I sighed.

"I've seen drawings, and read descriptions of creatures from hell," Malc carried on. "But actually seeing them for real is something else. I can't wait to find out how it got here."

"Nox said someone must have brought it here, or..." I didn't finish the sentence. Would Nox want Malc to know his power might be weakening?

"Or what?"

"Erm," I said.

"Or his power might have weakened enough that one

escaped?" Malc peered intensely down the camera at me. I swallowed awkwardly. "It's okay. I know that giving up the sins weakened him."

"Oh. Good," I said. He obviously didn't know that passing his power to me through some sort of cray sex-curse-magic might have weakened him further.

"Well, our list in't getting any smaller, Beth. We still have,"—he held up his fingers and began to cross them off as he listed our tasks—"Alex's murder, the Book of Sins, Sloth's page, and Envy and Pride's whereabouts to investigate."

All before we can get to my parents, I added silently in my head.

My usual positivity was missing today, I realized as I stared glumly down at my notepad. Being attacked by a lethal hell creature appeared to have put a dampener on my spirits.

"Oh, speaking of which..." He spun back to his laptop and started typing as he spoke. "I got something from one of Alex's neighbors. I hacked Inspector Singh's computer, and she had a few witness statements. This one was interesting."

One of the screens in front of us filled with typed text. I scanned it quickly.

'Neighbor recalls seeing a man outside the victims apartment who she described as "a big bloke in a long coat and a dodgy hat." She didn't see his face and said she wouldn't recognize him again if she saw him.'

. . .

I chewed on my lip, thinking. "A big bloke. That could be anyone."

"Except a small woman," Malc grinned at me.

"Do you think we should go and see this neighbor?"

Malc shook his head. "Nah. She said she wouldn't recognize him again, and she never saw his face. It does narrow the field a little though. I guess we can rule out Wrath."

I shook my head. "She could have got her pet demon, Cornu, to go. He's big." I felt a tinge of heat creep into my cheeks when I realized what I'd said, and I'd seen the demon naked.

My desk phone rang and I picked it up gratefully.

"Do you fancy a trip to Solum this afternoon?" Nox's husky voice sounded no less appealing on the telephone.

"Yes. Definitely. But I won't be getting any further with this mountain of things to investigate if I'm off roaming London with you."

"Well, I have a new lead. My brothers want to meet me. They claim to know something the Ward does, and that we don't. About Alex's murder."

"Your brothers? As in, the ones who apparently want to go to war with you?"

"Yes. Though Michael claims that isn't true. We will meet them and gauge the truth of it ourselves."

"We?"

"Yes. Saturday night. Which is why we must visit our

friendly neighborhood genie today. I'll tell you more when we're not on the phone."

"You need to hide my wings?" I looked uncertainly at Nox in the back of the towncar. Claude's car was becoming something of a safe haven for me. A quiet, private place where it seemed Nox and I had a lot of our important conversations.

"Yes. I do not want my brothers to know that you have any of my power. Of course, they are very powerful angels, and may sense it in you anyway, but I am hoping not."

"I can't see my wings," I said, leaning over my shoulder and peering at nothing. Every now and then something caught a slight fluttering of light, but I couldn't make out actual wings. "I can't feel them or anything. Have they got more visible since... last time?"

"No, I don't believe so. Only those with a lot of magic can see them. My brother's fall into that category."

"How did I see them the first time?"

"I imagine it has to do with the fact that the power had just entered your body." His expression shifted, and I squirmed a little. "They're quite beautiful. Delicate, careful. Like you."

I moved to kiss him, but caught myself. "I'm not sure how careful I am these days."

"I warned you the devil's influence may rub off on you," he smiled.

I bit the inside of my cheek. "As we're going to Solum already," I started, steeling myself. "I would like to see the genie and do the blood tests."

Light flared in Nox's eyes. "I am very glad to hear that."

"I think we need to know as much as we can about the curse," I said, not adding the real reason, which was that I was desperate to be able to kiss him and if the genie could do anything at all to make that possible again, I would try it.

"I agree." His eyes were boring into mine, his look a promise of the fulfillment of a million desires I never knew I had.

He knew exactly what my motivations were.

NINETEEN

BETH

It turned out that it was Adstutus that Nox had wanted to go see anyway, so it was an ideal time to offer myself up for the genie's tests.

"I must confess to being curious about your situation myself. I am glad you have opted to find out more," Adstutus said to me, before rolling up my sleeve. He was wearing a Guns and Roses t-shirt this time, and his little shop smelled like frankincense. It reminded me a bit of the retirement home.

It was a surreal experience, sitting in the Arabian tent style room, a genie poking a very non-magic needle into my arm. But I focused on the conversation Nox and Adstutus were having and tried to ignore it.

"I can definitely make you a potion that will keep any magic at all from emanating from her. Although I have to be honest, I can't sense very much myself, so I don't think you need to worry."

"I wouldn't be asking you if there was no need," Nox said tersely.

"No, I suppose you wouldn't. Fine, I'll make you something. You can pick it up tomorrow."

"Thank you. Send the invoice to Rory."

"I will do. Nice girl."

I pulled a face. I would never have described Rory as a 'nice girl'.

"Now, please can we get you back to the well before you leave?" the genie asked me as he finished with my arm and put a tiny pink plaster on the little hole in my skin.

"Sure." My stomach fluttered nervously at the thought of seeing those gold wings behind me again. But there was something alongside the nerves. Something a little excited.

I mean, it was magic. Real-life magic, and it was in me. It was hard not to feel a touch like a storybook character.

I stood over the glassy liquid, and again felt that bold shot of magic from Adstutus.

I watched, breathless, as the wings appeared behind me, bright and gold. More shadow than last time seemed to swirl across them, and the bolt of electricity-type power that made them vanish was so much stronger than the first time that I actually stumbled.

Nox caught me, and glared at the genie.

"What happened?" he barked.

The genie gave him a look that put me in mind of my

most severe school teachers preparing to give their students hell.

"She has more of your power now. That is what happened."

Nox held his accusatory glare, but I couldn't. "We didn't have sex," I protested in a small voice.

"Then you engaged in some sort of other activity that passed power between you?" He raised his eyebrow high.

"Erm. It was a sex based activity."

"As I thought." He tutted. "The willpower of a human I can understand waning, but you should know better," he said to Nox.

"I will tell you once again, I care nothing for your lectures, old man. I will be by tomorrow for the potion, and inform me at once if you learn anything from the blood tests."

"Arrogant fucking genie," Nox muttered when we left.

"He does kind of have a point. It was a bit irresponsible of us to, erm, test the curse."

"We are grown adults, and it was our own risk to take." He stopped walking, and pulled me to face him. "Do you regret it?"

"No." I didn't.

"Nor do I. So we move on. Coffee?"

Once installed in the same bench seat at the window of the fancy coffee shop, I did actually feel a bit more hopeful. Watching the patrons of the Solum bazaar was utterly fascinating. I saw a man about three feet taller than everyone else with a faint green cloud shimmering around him. Everyone was giving him a wide berth.

"What is he?" I asked Nox.

"Troll."

"Troll? I thought they were ugly?" The tall man was far from ugly, though he wasn't conventionally good looking. More like lumberjack-hot.

Nox shrugged. "Some are. Are you attracted to him?" Something dangerous gleamed in his eyes, and my body responded not with indignation but with pleasure. I wanted him to be jealous.

"He stands out," I said casually. I was playing with fire, and I knew it.

The troll stumbled, and people scrambled to get out of his way as it looked like he was going to fall over. He righted himself, though, glaring from side to side as though something had tripped him.

I turned to Nox, my mouth open. "Did you do that?"

"It's not my fault if the creature can't put one foot in front of the other."

"You did, didn't you?"

Tendrils of smoky energy whispered around him and he gave me a sultry smile. "If he can't manage his feet properly, I doubt he would be very adept with his hands."

My mind filled with memories of Nox's hands, touching and stroking my skin, moving closer and closer to my aching core. His fingertips whispering over my panties.

I glared at him. "You've made your point."

He said nothing, but drained his coffee cup.

After another ten minutes of magical-people watching, he spoke. "I know you are still feeling the after-effects of yesterdays attack, but I am afraid I can't delay investigating Alex's death. I had planned to pay a visit to the wolf pack this afternoon." My gut tightened at the mention of Alex and wolves. "I understand if you sit this one out."

"Do you want me to come?" I asked him. I already knew I was going. Tired and glum or not, I wasn't going to miss both a chance to find out more about the murder, and a chance to meet werewolves. But I wanted to hear his answer.

"Yes. You knew Alex well, which may help. And we agreed to undertake this together."

"I'll come."

"Good. Know that I will protect you if anything goes awry. Wolves are dangerous, but you will be safe with me."

I cocked my head at him. The irony was, I had been in more danger since I had met him than I ever had been in my life. And he was the one taking me to more dangerous places.

I thought back to the hellhound the night before, and my instinctive reactions. Sure, there had been the initial bolt of fear that had frozen me, but it had passed. I hadn't stayed rooted to the spot, or started screaming or crying. Was that because I knew Nox was there and that he would protect me? Or was it because I had some faith in myself now? Nox hadn't saved me from Max, I'd done that myself.

"Thank you," I told him. "You know, I'd like to get good at protecting myself."

He looked at me thoughtfully. "Rory is an expert in martial arts."

"What?"

"Martial arts needs no magic, but could be very useful for both defense and attack."

"You're not suggesting Rory would teach me?"

"Why not?"

"She hates me!"

"Really?" Nox looked surprised.

"Yes."

"I suppose she hates most people," he mused. "I could tell her she has to teach you. I am her boss."

"Yeah, that would make for some super fun lessons," I said sarcastically. "I'll see if I can bring it up with her," I said. "And if not, I'll look into classes elsewhere."

It wasn't actually a bad idea at all. If I was going to be a part of this new world of champagne and corpses, then the ability to land a few decent kicks on an opponent might well come in useful. Maybe not against a hellhound, but enemies came in all shapes and sizes.

TWENTY

BETH

As we finished our coffees, Nox filled me in on the way werewolves worked.

"They are pack animals, and they have an Alpha, and a Beta. They will always do what their Alpha commands, without exception," he told me.

"Even if they don't want to?"

"Yes. Which is good for the Ward in some ways because it means as long as they have the Alpha in check, everyone else behaves."

"And how is it bad?" I asked.

"Everyone wants to be the Alpha. Challenges are regular and messy."

"Oh."

"The current Alpha of this pack won his place just a couple months ago. He's known to be much more aggressive than the last few, which is why I had already been keeping an eye on him."

"How many packs are there?"

"Three in London. And the one we're interested in is called Mordere pack. The biggest and baddest. And they frequent the Moon and Fiddle."

"The Moon and Fiddle?"

"A pub. In Solum."

"That's where we're going next?"

"It sure is."

The pub looked like any normal British pub from the outside, other than the fact that it was in the middle of a magical bazaar. A board hung from the beams decorating the building, showing a full moon and the silhouette of a fiddle in front of it. I was sure I had seen other pubs in London with the same name. I doubted they were full of werewolves, though.

Nox entered first, and I took a deep breath before I followed him, unsure what to expect.

The first thing I noticed was that it was packed with people. Every table in the cramped, cottage-style room was full. The low bar at the far end was lined with customers. The second thing I noticed was the smell. A faint wet dog scent permeated the air, along with the sweeter smell of beer.

All eyes snapped to Nox as the door swung closed behind us. A few pairs of eyes darted to me, but none lingered. I guessed the devil was of far more interest than I was. The loud conversations died down to a hush as Nox took a step into the crowded room. I followed him, the old-fashioned burgundy carpet oddly springy beneath my feet.

"Good day. Is Jaxon here?" Nox asked mildly, looking around the pub. A well-built man stepped away from the bar, tilting his head in a distinctly predatory movement as he faced us. His nostrils flared in his hard, weathered face. I didn't think he was older than forty. Scruffy blond hair fell over his forehead, and he had a short beard.

"Take a seat," he said after a pause, and gestured to a table where two women and a much younger man were seated. They stood up immediately, picking up their pints and moving to the wall.

"Thank you," Nox said, and made his way to the table.

"And you'll be drinking what?" The man asked him.

"Scotch, and a gin for my friend."

A gin sounded like a good idea, I thought as I moved to take the seat next to Nox. A low-level anxiety was rumbling through me, making me concentrate hard on everything around us.

A hum of conversation rose back up as the man turned back to the bar, but the eyes didn't leave us. I took the opportunity to study the guy's back. He was wearing ripped jeans and a tight t-shirt, and his whole body was wrapped in tightly packed muscle. I could see white scars all over his exposed arms as he turned back to us, carrying a beer. A small girl, who looked too young to be in a pub, hurried after him with a whiskey and a gin and tonic.

"So. What does the devil want with Mordere pack?" Jaxon said as he sat down.

"You know a man named Alex Smith?"

"Sure."

I sat up straight.

"How do you know him?"

"He was banging that Sarah chick from the Aphrodite Club."

I reached for my drink.

"That doesn't answer the question," said Nox.

Jaxon sighed and took a swig of his beer, before leaning back in his chair. "Sarah used to bang one of ours. When he heard that Alex could see behind the Veil we decided to shit him up a little bit. That's all."

"Did you know he's dead?"

Jaxon shrugged. "Yeah, that wanker from the Ward has been sniffing around. I'll tell you what I told him. It's nothing to do with us."

"Did he tell you that it looked like an animal attack?"

"So what? And why the fuck are you interested?"

Nox stiffened. "My business is none of yours."

Jaxon snorted. "Then why the hell should mine be yours?"

Power flared from Nox, heat and shadows coiling off his pristine suit. "You know very well why."

Jaxon leaned forward, elbows on the table. I could see the feral warning spark in his eyes, and a faint glow came off his own tanned skin. "Look, rumor has it, you ain't all you used to be. Now, I have no quarrel with the devil, but I've no reason to sit here and defend myself to you."

I realized belatedly that the others around us had fallen quiet again. A low, rumbling growl came from somewhere behind us, and Jaxon threw a sharp glance over my shoulder. He gave a weird snapping sound, and the growl stopped.

"Rumors are often untrue," said Nox, his voice now gravelly and hard. "I am not your enemy. I just want to know who killed Alex."

"Why?" Jaxon folded his arms and stared at Nox. His meaning was clear. He wasn't giving up anything without something in return.

"He's doing me a favor," I said. "I knew Alex."

The Alpha's eyes locked onto mine, and a sense of intelligent, deliberate violence washed over me.

"I'm sure you did," he half purred. Heat pulsed from Nox, but he said nothing. "We chased him around a few days. Then he started moving further out of town, and we couldn't be fucked to go after him. It was a game. We never touched him."

"Further out of town? Where?" Nox snapped.

"I don't know, south somewhere. Beyond our borders."

The feeling of so many eyes on us made me glance over my shoulder, my skin prickling. I sucked in a breath as I realized that one of the spectators was a huge white wolf, sitting between two tables, yellow eyes glowing as it stared at us. Had the wolf been there when we came in, or had he shifted while we were talking?

I turned slowly back to Jaxon. He had a lazy grin on his face. "I can hear your heart pounding, and I can smell you," he said to me.

"Well, stop smelling me," I answered, before Nox could say anything.

Jaxon's grin widened. "If you don't want your scent taken then you'd better leave."

Leaving was starting to seem like a good idea. "Thanks for your time." I gave him a sarcastic smile and stood up, draining my drink as I did. The fizzy tonic made my eyes sting and I slightly regretted the cocky maneuver.

"You're welcome," Jaxon answered in a mocking voice, standing at the same time as Nox. He, too, tipped back the rest of his drink, then threw a glare at the Alpha and strode to the door, holding it open for me.

It was a relief to be back outside, the feeling of being watched falling away as we moved further from the pub, toward the busier part of the bazaar.

"Do you believe him?" I asked as I trotted alongside Nox. He was walking fast, which I guessed was because he was pissed.

"Annoyingly, yes. The man is an asshole, but I don't think he is lying."

"Yeah, that's what I thought too. What did he mean by borders? And me not wanting my scent taken?"

"The three packs have borders, which they don't cross. And if a wolf takes your scent he will be able to find you easily."

I shuddered. "I don't want him, or anyone else in that room, to be able to find me."

Nox stopped striding along the cobbles and turned to me. "I will remove any mark any wolf ever puts on you," he growled.

"I, erm, appreciate that," I told him, unsure what else to say.

He just nodded and resumed his stride.

He was silent the rest of the way back to the car, and I laid a hand on his arm once we joined the line of traffic that led back to the office.

"You okay?"

"I wish it was him. I am annoyed that it isn't." Shadows were swimming in his eyes.

"I know what you mean. Maybe it was a hellhound then?"

"I thought about that. There was no evidence of fire or burning at Alex's flat. There would have been, if it was a hellhound attack."

"Huh. Good point."

Back to square one on Alex's murder, then.

Nox huffed out an angry breath. "We will review all footage anywhere near Sloth's shithole spa around the time he lost the page."

"Okay. Does that mean you're going to come and help me out in the research department? My office isn't as nice as yours." I said the words teasingly, trying to ease his temper.

It worked. The shadows skittered away as he focused on me. "Then we will get you a nicer office."

I laughed. "It will be nicer for having you in it."

Desire flashed over his features. "I would have you in a heartbeat," he rumbled.

"That's not what I meant," I said, but the words were hollow. A surge of frustration welled up in me and we fell quiet.

"Do you want to stay with me tonight?" he asked, as the enormous walkie-talkie building finally came into view. "In the guest room, of course. I don't think it is safe for you to be alone until we find out why the hellhound attacked."

"We may have to sit ten feet apart, and ban certain words," I said.

"Certain words?"

"Yes. The ones that make my insides do funny things. Don't pretend you don't say them like that on purpose."

"Words like *temptation*?" he said, slowly and deliciously.

"Yes. Words exactly like that," I said, reaching out and punching him in the arm.

"Fine. I won't say anything like temptation."

"Seriously? Stop saying it!"

He smiled wickedly at me as the car pulled up to the curb. "You may have to bring Monopoly."

TWENTY-ONE

BETH

Nox clearly did not expect me to actually have Monopoly tucked under my arm when Claude dropped me at his house later that evening. I waved it at him as soon as he opened the grand front door and surprise flickered in eyes, replaced quickly by amusement.

"You realize I will beat you."

"You can't cheat," I said, moving past him into the house. "I'm used to playing with Francis, so I know all the usual methods."

"I'm quite sure I have plenty of methods you don't know about," he said, and I didn't think he was talking about Monopoly anymore.

I took my boots off, Beelzebub charging over to me as soon as I crouched down. "Maybe you can be banker, huh?" I said to the dog as he wagged his tail happily against the shining wood floor. "Sort out any arguments before they happen?"

Huge puppy eyes stared up at me, and his tongue lolled out of his mouth before he jumped, trying to lick my cheek.

I laughed. "Maybe not."

"I thought we might have takeout tonight," Nox said.

"Great."

"Thai okay?"

"Definitely," I replied as I followed him to the kitchen. I could get used to the menu that came with spending time with Nox, for sure.

"Want to see a new room?" he said, turning to me suddenly.

Hell yes, I did. The house was massive, and I'd only seen about five rooms so far.

I followed him to the stairs that led to the roof terrace, but instead of exiting we carried on up, into the rear wing of the house. On the next floor, he stepped off the staircase onto a landing and pushed open one of two doors.

We entered a formal dining room, the far wall all glass, looking down over the swimming pool and glittering deck. The dining table was laid cleanly with white cloth and crockery, a single yellow rose in the center. Tall, art deco style Tiffany lamps lit the room, displaying thick-stroked abstract oil paintings in pastel colors on the walls.

It managed to be both modern and distinctly retro all at the same time.

"Will this do, for dinner and board games?"

"It's perfect."

. . .

Annoyingly, Nox was better at Monopoly than me. And I was fairly confident he wasn't cheating.

The food had been delicious, as had the wine Nox paired with it, and I wondered if the alcohol had affected my ability to master the real estate game.

"I concede," I said eventually, huffing out a sigh and dragging my eyes off the game board. I couldn't win.

A wicked gleam of satisfaction shone in his eyes from across the table. My suggestion of staying ten feet apart hadn't been such a silly one - we were at least five feet apart and I hadn't thrown myself at him yet.

And he hadn't said any outrageously sexy words. In fact, he hadn't said many words at all.

"Nox, tell me something about yourself."

"You already know my favorite color."

"Yes, I do. Tell me something else."

He leaned back in his chair, and pulled a thoughtful face, his eyes not leaving mine. "I prefer chess to Monopoly."

I snorted, then wished I had made a more ladylike noise. "You'll have to find someone else to play chess with. I don't know the rules."

"I'll teach you."

"Okay. Once we've sorted our current mess out, I'll learn chess," I said.

"Our current mess being our inability to have sex?"

He asked mildly, but I glared at him. "That's a forbidden word," I told him. "But yes. That and *you* being a murder suspect this time."

His face darkened. "I hope that if nothing else, the meeting with my brothers will shed some light on that."

"About your brothers," I said. "You said, a while back, that they were connected to the Ward?"

"Yes. They have a hand in running it. Since I stepped down."

"Right. And, erm...why am I coming, exactly?"

"Michael asked me to bring you."

Nerves skittered through me. Wrath and Sloth were the only two other angels I had met, and it sounded like Nox's brothers were stronger than them. If they were as strong as Nox.... That would be a lot of angel aura in one place.

"Where are we meeting them?"

"The casino again. It's my ground, and now familiar to you."

My stomach sank. I felt so out of place there. My mood must have shown on my face.

"If you wish to purchase clothing you would feel more comfortable in, you can expense it. This is a business meeting after all," he said.

I opened my mouth to say *no, thank you* but paused. I remembered how much better I had felt around Nox when we very first went out to the Ivy, when I was dressed to impress. Wearing my girl armor.

And it wasn't like he couldn't spare the cash.

"I'm sure that would help, thank you," I said. A frisson of excitement at the notion of going clothes shopping ran through me. I loved shopping, but it was an activity I had partaken in very little the last few years.

This was a treat, and I was going to make sure I enjoyed it as one.

Once again, Nox read my mood perfectly. "I think we should end the evening with you looking forward to the morning." He smiled warmly and stood up.

A little stab of disappointment speared me, but he was right. We should go to bed now, before we got any closer.

"If you sleep any later, then you're doing this on your own." The cool British female voice stirred me from sleep. When my drowsy haze faded enough that I realized the voice was in the room with me, I sat bolt upright.

Rory was leaning against the bedroom doorframe, texting on her phone.

"What... Why are you here?"

"Apparently, we're going shopping." She gave me a look that said she'd rather gouge out her eyes with a spoon than shop with me.

I continued to stare blankly at her and she rolled her eyes. "When I dropped off Nox's clothes a few minutes ago, he said that it might be nice if I accompanied you to Oxford Street. I don't think it would be nice at all, but given that he's my boss, and I do actually like him, here I am."

She gestured to herself, then went back to her phone.

I would kill Nox. Why the hell had he suggested Rory come with me?

I thought back to the last conversation we'd had about the pixie-with-the-attitude-problem. He had been surprised that Rory didn't like me, and told me to ask her for self defense lessons. With a sigh I thunked my head back down on the pillow. I'd said I'd ask her if an opportunity came up. I hadn't expected him to create one.

"Will you please get out of bed, so we can get this over and done with."

I glared at Rory, then swung my legs out of bed. "I'll see you downstairs in fifteen minutes," I told her. She didn't even look at me as she pushed herself off the doorframe and left.

I checked out her outfit as she went. A bodycon black dress with cap sleeves and ankle boots. She looked great. Maybe she would be a good person to shopping with. Although I couldn't see her volunteering any helpful advice to little-old-me.

I showered as fast as I could, and pulled on black jeans and a blue t-shirt with cherries printed on the front. It was cutesy compared to what Rory was wearing, but that was why I picked it. I couldn't match her level of sass, so something entirely different was probably my best bet.

I swiped some make up on, and headed downstairs. Nox was in the kitchen, and he pushed a cup of coffee toward me as I entered. He was wearing a full suit and tie, and exuded wealth and confidence.

I took the coffee gratefully.

"It's cool enough to drink fast," he said, with a sideways glance toward the front door, where Rory must be waiting impatiently.

"Why did you ask her to take me shopping?" I hissed at him.

"Because I have to go to a board meeting today, and I didn't want you to be alone," he said quietly.

"So, she's my babysitter?"

"Think of it more like a bodyguard, if it makes you feel better."

I scowled. "It doesn't."

"Rory is well connected, good in a crisis, and stronger than she looks. Above all that, she is one of only two people I trust implicitly." I wondered who the other one was, but he didn't give me time to ask. "Have a good day. I'll see you here at seven." He leaned over the counter, pressing his lips to my cheek. Heat flared out from the contact, zips of electricity sparking through my chest.

I bit back a groan as my nipples hardened. With a last smoldering look, he left the kitchen.

I stared after him in a sex-daydream-daze, until Beelzebub head-butted my leg.

"Sorry boy," I muttered to him, bending and scratching his ears.

"If we could leave sometime this week, then that would be good!" called Rory from the hallway.

I looked down at the dog and he stared balefully back at me. "Wish me luck," I told him.

TWENTY-TWO

BETH

"Nope. Put it back." I gritted my teeth, but did as Rory said, sliding the long green dress back onto the rail I'd picked it up from.

"What's wrong with it?"

"Color's bad for you."

I turned to her, surprised to see that for the first time she didn't have her phone out.

"Really? I like green."

"Well, you're wrong. Blue is good on you." Her eyes flicked to my t-shirt. "Ice blue. Or purple. But purple without too much red in it."

"Oh. Right. Thanks."

I browsed the rails again, trying to find anything in the colors she'd mentioned. She sighed loudly.

"Come on."

"What?"

"Come on. This shop doesn't have what you need."

"But it's-" She held up a finger, at the same time as fisting her other hand on her hip, and I stopped speaking.

"Do you want my help, or not?"

I needed to look and feel not-helpless in the presence of three all-powerful angels. I needed all the damn help I could get.

"Yes. Please," I said.

"Then come on."

I followed her out of the store, then off Oxford Street altogether, onto Great Marlborough Street. She gestured at a massive Tudor style building with black beams and white render. It was beautiful, and I recognized it immediately.

"This is Liberty of London." I said, staring.

"And?"

"And I can't afford anything in there."

She rolled eyes yet again. "Number one, you're not paying. Number two, your wages went in this morning, so you probably could afford it, even if you were. Number three, it is the only shop in a mile vicinity where the staff are magic and can fucking see me - so take it or leave it."

"My wages?" I asked, zoning in on point number two. "But it's not the end of the month."

"Mr. Nox's special employees are paid weekly."

"Oh. And I was paid enough that I could afford *this*?"

Her lips pursed. "I'm assuming that he didn't give you a contract, as you appear to know nothing."

"No. He didn't."

"Arrogant fucking men," she muttered. "At least he wears it well."

She had a point, Nox did wear arrogance well. "He orders for me, too," I said.

She fixed her beautiful eyes on mine, assessing me. "Does he order shit you like?"

"Yes."

"Then let him."

"I'd kind of reached that conclusion too."

"Good. Now, let's buy a dress."

Rory was good at shopping.

We'd barely been in the store five minutes before she had a trail of salespeople running around after us, either looking for garments that matched her detailed criteria, or trying to find the right size in others that she had spotted.

It wasn't long before I was loaded into a changing room almost as big as my bedroom, with an arrangement of stunning dresses hanging before me.

"Try the royal blue floor-length first," Rory called. "I don't think it will work and I want to discount it early."

I did exactly as she told me to, and she was right. The royal-blue floor length didn't suit me. I left the changing room to show her anyway.

"Yup. I didn't think so," she said from the large armchair she was perched in. "Next." She waved her hand.

It took four more dresses until we found the right one, and I knew it before I showed Rory. It was pale purple and the bust was two sections of fabric over my shoulders and breasts, gathered into a high waistband, leaving an inch gap in the middle. It was way more cleavage than I would normally show, but I liked it. The skirt was knee length and full, making me want to spin around.

"Yes," said Rory as soon as I emerged from the curtain. "But you'll need a different bra."

I looked down at the bra strap showing in the middle of the plunging neckline. "That or go without," I said. She scowled at me.

"If you have an excuse to buy new underwear, take it."

I considered her words for just a few seconds before shrugging. "Why not?"

I was starting to enjoy this having-money thing.

We found a bra that was designed for exactly the kind of dress I was wearing. It had a tiny diamanté strap holding the cups together that was stronger than it looked and would look perfect between the sheaths of dress fabric.

Next, we found shoes with equally pretty diamanté straps, but they were considerably more uncomfortable than the bra. And somehow, cheaper.

"Who knew underwear cost more than shoes?" I murmured as we left the store. Rory looked at me like I was an alien.

"Everyone, Beth."

"Oh." I looked up and down the busy street, shoppers and tourists everywhere. "Is there anything you need to get?" I asked her.

"No. I'll call Claude," she said, pulling her phone from her purse.

"Well, thanks for your help."

Her eyes flicked to mine, and I tried to capitalize on her actually deigning to look at me. "I mean it - I would never have found this dress on my own. You have an amazing eye."

She said nothing for a long moment, and just as I was about to mentally abandon being nice to her, she coughed.

"You look good in it. I hope it helps."

It was far and away the nicest thing she'd said to me, and I had to make an effort to stay nonchalant. I didn't imagine she would appreciate a beaming smile from me. Smiling wasn't really her thing.

Claude pulled up in the towncar, saving us from any awkwardness.

"Have you met Nox's brothers?" I asked her, once we were inside.

"Yes."

"What are they like? Anything I should know first?"

"Powerful. Hot as hell. Holy as heaven, though." She pulled a face as she said the last sentence.

"Holy? As in how angels are supposed to be?"

"They work on the opposite of Nox's power. Good stuff. Kindness. Charity. Sacrifice. That sort of shit."

"Oh." My head tried to work that through. How could they be bad guys if that were true?

To be fair, Nox had never said they were bad guys, just that they didn't like him, and that they might be planning to go to war with him. It occurred dimly to me that Nox should most likely be considered the bad guy.

Swallowing my discomfort, and twenty-plus years of Christian preaching, I looked at Rory again. "Nox mentioned you knew self-defense."

She blinked at me. "I'm a black belt in three martial arts," she said slowly. "But I don't know what that has to do with anything."

"I, erm, well..." *Come on Beth, pull yourself together. She's not that terrifying.* "Would you possibly have time to show me some stuff? Just enough to get out of a bad situation, not help me get to black belt or anything."

She blew out a long breath. "Did Nox tell you to ask me?"

"Yes, he suggested it, but please don't say yes just because your boss wants you to." I held her gaze and made sure I spoke firmly. "I'm serious about learning to defend myself and I want to learn from someone who cares."

A flicker of surprise registered in her eyes. "Well, if you're serious...? I'll think about it."

"Thank you," I nodded. I wanted to get started as soon as I could, but learning from Rory would be better than anyone else - she would know exactly what sort of dangers someone who associated with Nox got into. Like hellhounds, crazy bird shifters, and angry Alpha wolves. "Champagne and corpses," I muttered.

"What?"

"Oh, nothing." She continued to stare at me, so I explained. "Champagne and corpses. If you want the

Champagne, you've got to deal with the corpses. That's what it's like, spending time with Nox."

She looked at me a while longer. "Maybe you're not as pathetic as I originally assumed," she muttered eventually, then went back to tapping on her phone.

It was pretty shit, as far as compliments went, but I planned to take that statement as a monumental leap in our relationship.

TWENTY-THREE

BETH

I was starting to think of the beautiful guest room as my own, I realized as I smoothed down my dress and looked in the mirror. There had been a tiny bottle and a note on the bed when I'd returned.

Beth, please drink this - it will hide your wings. See you at seven. Nox

There was a knock on the door, and I glanced at the stylish black clock on the wall. Seven exactly. My heart fluttered as I moved to open it.

I hadn't worn anything as daring as the low cut dress in front of Nox before - hell, in front of *anyone* before - and there was no point pretending I wasn't hoping for a reaction.

Boy, did I get one.

"You can't wear that." His voice was gruff, his eyes pinned to my chest and blazing with light.

"Erm, hello to you too," I said.

"I mean it, Beth. I need to concentrate tonight, and I can't do that when you look..." His eyes moved the rest of the way down my body, then back up to my face. "This fucking hot," he finished.

Pleasure radiated from my center, confidence billowing out with it. "Well then, you'll just have to work extra hard to focus. Because I'm wearing it. You were the one who suggested I go out and buy a dress."

He let out a hiss of air. "Because I thought it would make you feel better in my casino. Not because I wanted a rock-hard cock all night."

I felt my already rouged cheeks heat, and a pulse between my legs. My eyes darted to his crotch unbidden. He caught the look.

"Would you like proof of what you're doing to me?" he growled.

Yes. More than anything in the world. Take off your pants and show me that big, hard, perfect cock.

"No, thank you," I said, as my filthy thoughts made my cheeks burn. I kept my voice as airy as I could, but I feared it came out more breathless than aloof. "You look very nice too."

His jaw tightened, but he gave me a nod of thanks. He was wearing a black suit with a black tie. His eyes dipped to the string of jewels between my breasts. "Did you buy new underwear?"

I nodded.

Without another word, he whirled around, heading for the stairs.

"Well done, dress," I whispered, then patted the skirt appreciatively, and headed after him.

Nox sat as far from me as he could in the back of the car, and I would have taken offense if it weren't for the blatant desire written all over his face every time he looked at me.

"How was your meeting?" I asked him.

"Long."

"Oh."

"I can't see our wings. Did you drink the potion?"

"Yep. Tasted like strawberries." I smiled at him. He didn't smile back.

"Did you enjoy shopping?"

"Yes. Rory is extremely good at it."

"I've no doubt. Did you get a chance to bring up self-defense lessons?"

"Yes, I did. She said she would think about it. But Nox, please don't tell her to do it. I want to learn from someone who cares, not someone who is doing it out of obligation. If she doesn't want to do it, then I'll find a good teacher elsewhere."

"If that's what you want," he nodded.

"It is what I want. Thank you."

His look intensified, darkening and morphing into something bordering feral. "You do realize that right now I would do *anything* you want."

I gulped. "Anything?"

"Anything. For a taste."

"A taste of what?"

His eyes dipped, focusing first on my mouth, then my chest, then sliding down. I squeezed my thighs together. "You," he breathed. "A taste of you. I need something, Beth. Or I'm going to fucking explode."

My breath hitched higher, my pulse quickening. "Will a kiss be enough?"

"For now," he snarled, and in a movement so quick I had no time to prepare for it, my face was in his hands, and his ravenous mouth closed over mine.

A torrent of images flooded my head as he kissed me like a man possessed, his need evident in every sweep of his tongue, every nip of my lips, in the pressure of his hands on my skin.

Over and over I saw him in my mind, naked and glistening, his body entwined with mine and endless waves of pleasure engulfing us.

"Stop," I gasped, pushing him back. He moved with my hands immediately, his eyes wild and dark as they focused on mine. "We can't," I panted. "Not now, and not here. If we're going to be stupid enough to do this, we do it properly."

Blazing light flared in his eyes as he registered my words. "What are you saying?" Anger suddenly flickered across his face, and he moved farther back in his seat, away from me. "No, no, Beth, I'm sorry. We can't. We don't know the risk. I shouldn't have..."

Good lord, I wanted him. Painfully. But he was right.

We didn't know the risk. Perhaps if we did, we could decide if giving in was worth it.

"Adstutus should be in touch soon," I said quietly. "Then we'll know more."

Nox's expression softened, though I could still see the strain. "Yes. Let's hope so."

It was almost a relief to reach the casino. The tension between us was amped up so high you could burn yourself on the electricity in the air.

Nox opened the car door for me, formal and stiff, and I took his arm as we entered the building.

We made our way to the same back room where we'd met Madaleine, but instead of heading to the tables, we turned right, toward a bar. Cocktail glasses hung from a rail over the polished wood, and two men turned around on their stools as we approached.

If there were ever such a thing as an aura, these two had it. *In abundance.*

Power didn't roll in waves from them, like it did with Nox and Madaleine. It was more like they were the center of a giant cloud of it, gentle wafts of enticing energy drifting about them and tickling those in their vicinity.

The man on the left looked like he belonged on a Californian beach. A white t-shirt with a faded beer logo stretched across his broad chest, and he had long blonde hair tied at his neck in a ponytail. His tanned, chiseled face was more serious than his attire suggested though, his smile small and wary.

The man on the right, however, smiled so broadly that dimples showed in his dark cheeks. He had a mass of black messy curls on top of his head, the lower part shaved in a style that had only recently become trendy. He was wearing jeans, a white shirt, and a bright blue blazer, and he leaped up from his seat as we got close, his laughing eyes fixing first on me, then Nox. When he was only a foot from us, an excitable amusement took me, and I found myself wanting to laugh with him, though I had no idea what about.

"Brother," he said, reaching forward and pulling Nox into a hug that wasn't returned in the slightest. Nox didn't even let go of my arm. "And Beth Abbott," the man said, releasing Nox and gesturing both arms widely at me. "A pleasure to meet a woman so rare as to hold Lucifer's attention."

It threw me, hearing Nox referred to as Lucifer, and I fumbled my reply. "I, erm-"

"I'm so sorry, I haven't introduced myself," he said, saving me from finding the right words. "I am Michael. And this is my brother, Gabriel."

Gabriel sauntered over with his drink. Images of the beach, serene and calm and beautiful, floated through my mind.

"It's a pleasure to meet you," he said, and held out his hand. I shook it, and then he offered it to Nox, who eyed it a moment and then shook it too.

"Brother, I love what you've done with this place,"

said Michael cheerfully. "There's so much delicious excitement here."

"Never mind that it's tempered with loss, disappointment, and fear," muttered Gabriel, before taking a long swig of beer.

"Now now, you know there can't be one without the other. The world is about balance, dear Gabriel," Michael said, looking between the other two men. His accent was British, whilst Gabriel's was an odd mix I couldn't place. Maybe Australian. "Shall we take a seat?"

TWENTY-FOUR

BETH

We all sat at a table directly in front of the bar that had already been laid with food and drinks. I was only seated for a moment before realizing that the sound of the other patrons had dulled to muffled hum.

"We will not be overheard," smiled Michael.

"Right," I said, leaning over and swiping one of the champagne flutes. The dress was good, but a couple swigs of alcohol couldn't hurt to make sure I had what I needed to hold my own with these three.

"You're human," said Gabriel, and I looked at him. He was sitting opposite me, Nox to my right and Michael to my left.

"Yes."

"Brave, brother," he said, glancing at Nox.

"Brave?" I asked, confused. I was pretty sure nobody needed to be brave to interact with me.

"Mortal lifespans," said Michael. "It doesn't usually

end well."

"We are not here to talk about Beth," said Nox. He seemed calm, no raging heat spilling from his skin, so I took my cue from him and tried to relax a little.

"No, but it is so rare to see you with company," Michael beamed. "I'm happy for you, brother."

"That is not what Examinus would have me believe."

Gabriel rolled his eyes, leaning an elbow on the table. "Examinus is a fool. He is bored with his position in hell."

"I know the feeling," Nox ground out.

A look passed between the other two angels. "Whatever he has told you about us, it is not true. But we do wish to see you returned to power, Lucifer."

"Why?"

"The Ward only has so much power. The longer the sinners go unpunished by an entity that they truly fear, the more daring the sinners become."

Michael said the word sinners as though it tainted his tongue.

"Why don't you volunteer?" Nox fixed his eyes on him, and I felt the first tendril of heat.

"You know it doesn't work like that."

"I know nothing of the sort. I have proven that power can be transferred."

My stomach clenched for a moment at his words, and then I realized he meant the sins and the book, not me.

"Lucifer, you were born to this role. You are the overseer of sinners. The punisher of evil."

"I am a fallen angel," Nox growled. "With a role bestowed upon him. I am done with spending every waking hour of my life having the scum of the earth paraded before me. I've taken my turn."

"And now you ask me to fall? To take your place?"

Nox hissed out air. "You are supposed to be capable of empathy. Of selflessness. I dare you, brother. Take a turn in the role you beg me to return to."

Gabriel straightened as Michael's eyes flashed with something dark. His shoulders had gone rigid, his easy smile no longer seeming genuine. "Lucifer, the world needs you. Whether or not it is fair that the burden of your role should fall on one being's shoulders is not the point. That can not be changed. You have the capacity to contain more power than any of us. You were built to be the punisher."

Nox moved slowly to face him. "I have heard this lecture many times, Gabriel. What makes you think I will respond differently this time?"

"The Ward."

"You mean the organization you as-good-as run? What about them?"

"We do not run it, we oversee it. And the organization knows that they are failing. They do not believe that the increased number of crimes is due to their inability to create compliance. They believe that your power is not properly contained, and that is causing the creation of more sin."

Nox shrugged. "I don't give a shit what they believe. You have influence, whip them into shape. Hire more Wardens."

"I'm not sure that they don't have a point," said Michael.

"What?"

"I heard a hellhound made it into London."

A tense silence fell over the table, and I was sure everyone could hear my heart pounding. I felt like I was eavesdropping, hearing a conversation that I shouldn't be. I knew that Nox hated being the devil, that he didn't want the responsibility, but to hear him talk about it so bitterly... I felt for him on a gut-deep level. And more, I resented these two, marching around, telling him he should just sort his shit out and get on with it, without apparently a care in the world about what it did to him. Their own brother.

"There was a hellhound. Yes." Nox was terse. A little more heat was pulsing from him, but his eyes were normal. I moved my hand, closer to where his rested on the table. I didn't want to make him look weak, or like he needed me, but the impulse to remind him that he had an ally here was strong.

His hand moved to mine, our skin touching.

"I believe it was let out deliberately."

"By whom?"

"I don't know. I would guess the same person behind the theft of the Book of Sins, and the Sloth page."

An uneasy tension washed around us, and I wished some of the calming lounge music was audible through our magic bubble.

"I can assure you, brother," said Michael. "We have had nothing at all to do with any thefts. And the idea of intentionally releasing a hellhound into London is abhorrent." His smile had vanished completely now. "Unless you can prove that it was released deliberately, the Ward will believe that it is due to your waning power, leaking into this world."

"And that is at best," Gabriel added. "At worst, they will believe that you are deliberately causing sinful crimes."

Now Nox's face did tighten, and the hand touching mine flashed hot. I flinched, but kept my hand beside his. "They are sore losers. It has been decades since I toyed with them. They should move on."

"Lucifer... They found a feather at the scene of that boy's death."

An icy finger traced its way down my spine.

"What?"

"Alex Smith," said Michael. "They found a golden angel feather."

I turned my head to Nox at the same time he turned to me. "I did not kill him," he said, his voice low and intense, the words meant for me. He gripped my hand, hot energy sparking from him. "You know I can use the power of lust to bare my soul. Feel the truth of my words."

He lifted my hand to his lips, an urgent desperation in his face.

Certainty flooded me, compounding the knowledge I already had. Nox did not kill my ex-boyfriend.

"I didn't think for a second you did," I whispered.

Relief washed over his face, then his expression hardened.

"This has to do with Max." He turned to his brothers. "We were able to catch the thief who stole my book because he dropped a feather in my office. This must be connected. I'm being set up. Caught by a fallen feather."

Gabriel and Michael both stared, Gabriel thoughtful, Michael's face unreadable.

"It is possible," said Gabriel eventually.

"Possible? You actually think there's a chance I killed this man?"

"He was sexually involved with Beth," said Michael, pointing at me. "Wrath, envy, and pride could all motivate a killing like that."

"Three fucking sins I gave up," Nox snarled. "I will not sit here exchanging words with those that believe me guilty of crimes I did not commit."

He stood up, pushing his chair back loudly and taking my hand with him. I stood too, doing my best to look affronted on his behalf. It wasn't difficult.

"We are just trying to warn you, Lucifer," said Gabriel.

"Warn me of what? The Book of Sins has been stolen, someone sent a hellhound to attack us, and Examinus believes you two are part of an impending war against hell. Did you think I wasn't aware of the shitstorm coming my way?"

"If you had all of your power, you would be able to weather any storm that came your way, brother."

"Fuck you, Michael. Unless you want to take the

power of the devil, stay the fuck out of my life, or keep the Ward off my fucking back."

When I'd seen Nox angry before, he had become severe and clipped, as though straining to contain himself. But now, his Irish accent was thicker than I'd ever heard it, and his cursing somehow made him seem younger. No less powerful or dangerous, but somehow more human than godly.

"Goodbye then." Michael folded his arms, not even a ghost of his warm smile left.

Nox turned, and I turned with him.

TWENTY-FIVE

BETH

Nox didn't make for the town car when we got outside, stopping instead on the sidewalk and glaring around at vaguely startled customers entering the casino.

"Do... Do you want to walk?" He was still holding my hand, and I squeezed it as I spoke.

He looked at me, and I couldn't help stepping into him. I kissed him gently, not at all like the starved passion that fueled our earlier embrace. I needed him to know I was on his side.

He tensed for a moment and then relaxed into me, lifting a hand to my hair. He eased me back too soon.

"Yes. Please."

"Do you want me to walk with you?"

He nodded.

. . .

"Families, huh?" I said, as we strolled down the street. Shop windows were bright, and tourists and locals alike stumbled from bar to bar as cars crawled past us between stoplights.

"They're not my brothers in the same way that you would have siblings."

"No?"

"No. We were not born but created. I just happened to be created from the same batch of magic as them."

"Batch?"

"Magic is like energy. It can't be created or destroyed —it is infinite. It just moves from one thing to another if it is not used correctly. Stored, dormant magic can be resurrected. And in big enough bursts, it can create life."

"Wow."

"Hmm."

"Nox?" I said his name because I knew he would look at me, and he did. "I want you to know that I get it. I get why you gave up your power, and I don't think it's fair that you should be burdened with so much. I think..." I gazed at him, our pace slowing almost to a stop. "I think we should change something on our list."

He raised an eyebrow, eyes stormy with emotion. Good or bad, I couldn't tell. "Our list?"

"Yes. One, find the sin pages. Two, find the book. Three, find out who killed Alex - which has now morphed into clear your name of murder." Clear anger flicked over his face at that. "Four, break your curse and avert a war between the gods."

"The war my brothers say is not happening."

"Regardless, that's the one we have to change." We had stopped walking now. I took his other hand. "We need to find a way to keep your grumpy god happy and break your curse without taking your power back. It's not right, and even your brothers know that." Nox started to shake his head, but I clenched his hands. "Nox, don't write off what I'm saying yet. You gave your sins to fallen angels who weren't all as strong as each other, right? Like Madaleine is clearly strong, but Sloth is not."

"Yes, but—"

I didn't let him finish.

"It's clear your brothers won't take any of the power, but what if you found better angels to host the sins, and instead of you all being separate, you worked *with* the Ward doing whatever punishing needed to be done? As a team?"

I could see the refusal on his face. "I don't work well with others, Beth. And that wouldn't make Examinus lift the curse. He doesn't care about the Ward, he cares about being able to take advantage of my power." He let out a long breath. "I am one of the most powerful angels who has ever existed." His eyes dropped to the ground. "Or I was, anyway."

I screwed my face up. "Okay, well maybe that's not the answer then. But there must be something we can do."

"Beth, my brothers are right. That's why they piss me off so much."

"What do you mean?"

"I was created to punish people. If I don't do it, the

power of sin will end up out of control. I am the only one who can do it."

My shoulders sagged. He said the words with such finality.

"But maybe..." This time he squeezed my hands. "Maybe if I had all my power back, forced to spend my days dealing with the world's biggest assholes, it wouldn't be so bad as before."

"What would be different?"

"I don't know. Maybe nothing. Maybe everything."

His look was piercing, and I didn't know if I was being an idiot thinking he might be talking about me. Could I be the difference? I mean, I'd only known him a few weeks.

"You realize that's annoyingly cryptic?" I said, trying to lessen the intensity.

"Strategically cryptic," he corrected me, a gleam of his usual cockiness returning.

"Huh."

"I don't want to scare you."

I gave one of my unladylike snorts by accident. "Nox, you're way beyond scaring me."

He gave me a dark look. "I think could scare you without fire and shadows."

I gulped. I didn't doubt it.

"You know, my brothers were right about something else too."

"Oh yeah?"

"Yes. Angels and humans have some issues with dating over the long term."

My heart fluttered in my chest. *Long term.* Maybe I *was* the difference he had just alluded to.

I avoided looking at him as I answered. "Once we've lifted your curse, we might feel differently about each other." Which was code for *'once you can sleep with anyone you want instead of just me, you'll likely lose interest'*.

"Here's an idea. How about we add a new item to our list. Number five, work out how to make Beth live longer. Just in case."

My jaw slowly dropped open as my head snapped up to face him. "Are you serious?"

"Yes. There are many magical artifacts in this world. There must be something, or someone, who can help."

"Woa now, you don't just talk about making a girl immortal without asking her first."

His mouth quirked into a smile. "I'm sorry. Beth, please can I try to find a way to make you live longer?"

"I'm going to have to get back to you on that," I said, dropping one of his hands so that we could resume walking, a restlessness taking hold of me.

He chuckled, the sound rich and delicious and so different to that of Michael's. "Good answer. Do you know how rare it is to see so little greed in a human as there is in you?"

I looked sideways at him as we walked between tall iron-barred gates and entered the park. "I learned what value stuff had to me when I lost my parents. I'm no saint, I assure you."

"The hardest lessons in life are often the most

useful," he said quietly.

"And they can be forgotten," I muttered. "I'd be lying if I told you I didn't love the lifestyle you lead. This dress, your home, the food and wine... I love it."

"If luxury is not at the expense of others, you may enjoy it guilt-free."

"And you swear it isn't at the expense of others?" I stopped walking and looked at him. There was nothing around us but dark trees heavy with spring leaves, and the park lamplights were low.

"Beth, let me tell you something about myself, and the lessons I have learned," Nox said, staring back. "I am powerful enough to change the world. That is not an exaggeration. I have a temper than can end lives. I have a passion that can ruin minds. I have limitless desire. But it is not for the destruction of others or the ruination of happiness."

I saw the glimmering gold shape of his wings forming behind him.

"My position in the world is intrinsically linked to sin, to death and malice and pain, but those do not drive me. They do not scare me. They do not sadden me. That is not why I walked away. I abandoned my responsibilities because I wanted to find what was missing from my life. There is a gaping void inside me that I know will never be filled by hatred and sin. It took me centuries to recognize that I got no fulfillment from punishing scum. It took me several more to decide that what I wanted was more important to me than my responsibility. Selfishness drives me, Beth. I kill, but only those who deserve it. I steal, but only when it is due. I torment, but only those who made others suffer."

I realized I had been holding my breath as he paused, his eyes searching mine, blazing with light. His wings were gleaming brighter, expanding slowly.

"I do not benefit at the expense of others. But Beth, do not try to convince yourself that I am soft, or kind, or wholesome. I was not created that way. I was created to embody retribution, brutal and lethal."

He was godly. All encompassing, all powerful, and the most darkly beautiful thing that had ever existed.

I drew in his words, trying to piece them into my way of thinking, and failing.

He was a giant contradiction in my brain. I believed every word he'd said, yet I was totally and utterly drawn to him, trusting him with everything I had. I was not a person who could deal with someone who killed or tormented people. I was not a person who would choose to associate with someone intrinsically linked to sin, pain and death. But here I was, desperate to give myself completely to this person. To this fallen *angel*.

"Do you believe in retribution, Beth?"

I searched myself for an answer. "I believe in fair trials and second chances first." Shadows swirled between us, around us. "And I believe in you."

Heat coiled around me, a pressure drawing me closer to him. "You believe in me?"

"Yes. If you walked away from your responsibility then your reasons must have been sound to you. If you now wish to return, then you have new reasons."

"Perhaps I have found what was missing."

I was inches from him now, his murmured words sending caresses of breath across my own lips. "Nox, we barely know each other." My stomach was doing back-flips at his words, my excitement bordering on disbelief that he was talking about me in such a way. But my head had become louder than my heart over the last few years, and my fear lent even more volume.

Every doubt hammered through my mind in succession, holding me back from stepping fully into his embrace.

He may tire of me, when I am no longer his only option.

He may become a different person if he manages to regain his power.

The lure of him might not outweigh the life he described, one filled with pain and malice.

"We are more than passing acquaintances. We are more than one night. You are something to me Beth, and whilst I don't know what it is, I know that it is not fleeting."

He was right. I'd known it in my hospital bed, after Max almost killed me. Maybe I'd even known it before then.

We were bound, somehow.

"Take me home."

His wings curled around me, and he bent slightly to scoop me up in his arms. A delighted sound escaped me as I wound my arms around his neck, and he pulled me tight against his hard, hot body.

A thrill of anticipation made my skin tingle as his wings snapped taut, then beat hard. We rose, just a few inches off the ground. Nox's lips found mine for a brief, searing kiss, and then his great wings beat again.

This time we rose a foot.

Another beat, and another three feet.

Within seconds, we were high in the air, soaring over London. I pressed my face into his neck, looking over his shoulder. Moonlight made the swath of golden feathers shine brilliantly, and with each beat, his wings moved enough to expose the sight of the London skyline below. Bright lights against blackness, then glittering gold.

Wind rushed over the half of my face not protected by Nox's strong shoulder, and the cool sting made my skin feel even more alive than the adrenaline humming through my body.

It was so different to when he'd taken me from the boat, and dazed shock had kept all the exhilaration of flying from spilling over me.

I spotted the London Eye, pods bright, and then Wembley Stadium further out.

There were clouds around us, faint and wispy in the moonlight.

"This is amazing," I said, not knowing if Nox could hear me.

His arms gripped me tighter, and he changed our angle. Suddenly, we were moving fast, his wings tucking in slightly. Wind really rushed over me, and small squeak of delighted excitement escaped me as I buried my head behind his shoulders, only leaving my eyes peeking over.

Nox soared and dived and spun me around in the air, and I found myself disappointed when he finally descended toward a townhouse with a distinctive rooftop pool.

He set me down, and surprised me by stepping back immediately. "Beth, I can't tell you how much I want you."

"I want you too," I said, my chest heaving. Excitement and adrenaline were quickly melding into arousal.

"But until I know if being together might hurt you, I will not risk it."

I tried not to let the sting go too deep. He was absolutely right. We couldn't take the risk.

I nodded.

"We will go to Adstutus tomorrow. I will encourage him to work faster if he has nothing to share with us."

"Okay."

He reached out and stroked a thumb down my cheek, then tucked my windswept hair behind my ear. "Somebody has set me up for a fall, and I will not allow you to be harmed," he said softly. "I'm not risking anything when it comes to you."

TWENTY-SIX

NOX

I had already said too much.

I could see it in her eyes, hear it in her tone. Beth barely knew me, and I was talking about spending an eternal life with her. Making her life eternal.

I launched a fireball at the target at the far end of my basement. The mannequin exploded into fire. Not even a hint of satisfaction tremored through me. Nothing.

She wasn't scared of me, bizarrely. She was scared of something, though. Commitment? Magic? I looked down at my flaming fist. The world she would have to inhabit with me if I regained my powers?

I launched another fireball, the already charred mannequin on the right barely even catching light.

Somebody was setting me up for murder. The murder of her ex boyfriend. That man would have paid for his thieving, lying ways, I'd have made sure of it. The thought of him ever laying a hand on her made rage boil up through me, and I hurled two fistfuls of fire at the other end of the room. They hit nothing but the stone wall.

My need for Beth, my desire for her physically, grew daily. But my connection to her mind, my admiration for her strength and understanding - that grew *hourly*. In a world so full of judgement, and a culture so rife with selfish greed, she was a fucking beacon.

She could be the difference.

I needed her, to my core. Inside the flesh and blood that I was made of was a bond to her that was consuming my me.

Beth thought I had walked away from my responsibility because it was too much for me to bear. That I couldn't stand to punish all the worlds sinners.

She was wrong, and the need for her to understand that was painful. I would rather she thought well of me, because I wanted her to stay.

But what would happen when I was fully exposed to her? I couldn't stand the thought of her disappointment, of her fear. Better she knew now, and made her own choice.

I had given up my power to try to find what was causing the cataclysmic fucking boredom in my soul. The constant knowledge that there was something out there better than what I was doing. And I had found it. Found her.

Now, ironically, I had to take my power back to enjoy her. But how could Beth ever be happy at the side of a being who spent his days tearing sinners apart in hell?

Another double fireball blasted from my hands has impotent fury led my brain in circles. There was nowhere to go, no other option.

She couldn't. I wouldn't put her through that.

TWENTY-SEVEN

BETH

I was hoping like hell that the genie had come up with something useful when we stepped into his little shop the next day.

There had been a new tension between us when I'd entered Nox's kitchen that morning. His tone was stiffer, his flirtatious manner gone. As though even one misplaced word might cause us to do something stupid.

"Ah. Right on time," the genie said, as he materialized in the middle of the Arabic themed room.

"Really?" My hope that Adstutus could help was buoyed by the fact that he had been expecting us.

"Do you have news?"

"I do, Mr. Nox. I do." The genie gestured to me and I stepped toward him and the well. The smell of cinnamon was strong, an undercurrent of clove and antiseptic tickling my nose.

"Do you know how to stop Nox's power being transferred?" I asked.

"No. But I have a strong suspicion about why it is happening, and the outcome. From what I could see in the traces of power in your blood, I don't think Nox's power will harm you. The loss of it will continue to weaken him though. If you two continue to be intimate, you will draw all of his power, and you will become stronger. He, on the other hand, will wither into nothingness."

"I could kill you by having sex with you?" I looked in alarm at Nox.

"Not kill. Just weaken dramatically," said Adstutus.

"I don't want to weaken you," I said quickly. "I don't want to hurt you at all. Or take your magic."

"I know." Nox gave me a reassuring look, and then moved his eyes to the genie. "Let me guess why you think it's happening. Examinus. He made sure that if I were ever able to cheat the curse by being intimate, it would weaken me?" A resigned bitterness laced his words.

Adstutus nodded. "I believe that to be the most likely scenario."

"So, sex will hurt you, and not me. Your god seems like a real asshole." I sighed.

"He is."

"Please, if you want to blaspheme, do it elsewhere," the genie scowled at us, giving me a flashback of my mom's stern face.

"Can he hear us?"

"Examinus? Can he fuck. He's not as powerful as he thinks he is," rumbled Nox.

"Mr. Nox, please. Not here," Adstutus said again.

"Fine. Thank you for your time, Adstutus," Nox said, uncharacteristically polite to the genie. He didn't seem angry. Maybe he had been more worried about me getting hurt than him.

The genie hesitated, before holding up his hand.

"There is something else. It was very faint, and possibly nothing, but I did find traces of something else in Beth's blood. Other alchemists would have missed it, but I am supremely good." Adstutus face wore a mix of pride and serious misgiving.

I frowned, apprehension rebuilding from where it had just plummeted. "What did you find?"

"It looks like at least one of your parents was supernatural."

My heart stuttered.

"What?"

"You are definitely human, one hundred percent." He looked briefly at Nox before continuing. "There are very few beings who don't pass magic on by birth, but would be strong enough to leave traces of it in their offspring."

"Angels," breathed Nox.

I turned slowly to him as Adstutus nodded, my pulse now racing. What he had told me about angels not being born, but being created, tumbled through my mind. "My parents were angels? You can't be serious."

"The traces are too faint to be completely sure. But

angels are not able to pass magic on by birth, it must be bestowed on them. Vampires, for example, are the same, though they come into their magic other ways."

"Vampires?" My voice was as wobbly as I suddenly felt. Nox was at my side in an instant, and he put his arm around me. Warmth flowed into my body, steadying me.

"Vampires cannot reproduce," he said. His voice was grave. "Adstutus, what other beings are possible?"

"Right now I can think of none, other than angels. I will research further." The genie looked at me. "I am surprised that your parents never mentioned this to you."

"You and me both," I mumbled.

How could my parents be angels? *And not freaking mention it?*

The impact of what I'd just been told suddenly clicked into place.

"I knew it," I breathed. Nox raised an eyebrow. "I've known it for years, Nox, I just couldn't accept it. I knew magic and the supernatural existed. I knew my parents didn't just vanish." To both my and Nox's surprise, a laugh escaped my lips. "They're alive. Just not on Earth any more. Angels can leave this world, right? That's what you said?"

Nox nodded, a small smile crossing his tense features. "Angels are immortal, and they can move between realms." He stared intensely at me a long moment. Thoughts and emotions were rushing through my head at a million miles an hour, and I honestly couldn't work out what I was feeling.

"This is a lot, Beth. What do you need?"

I hesitated before speaking.

What did I need? I focused on the question, trying to pause the storm in my brain.

I needed something normal, something grounding. Something to offset the absolute madness that my life was becoming.

My little apartment and Francis had been the best part of my life for the last five years and it was them that cut through the tidal wave of crazy. "I'd like to go to Lavender Oaks Retirement Home, please."

TWENTY-EIGHT

BETH

"Whoa, whoa, whoa. Honey, did you hit your head?" Francis stared wide-eyed at me from the wooden bench we were sitting on. We were in the grounds of the retirement home, far away from prying ears.

"No. I had a blood test done by a genie, and he thinks my parent are angels."

I took a deep breath after repeating the statement to her.

It was necessary to say it out loud. I needed to keep saying it out loud.

If this revelation hadn't occurred after so much evidence of magic, Nox, and shifters and hellhounds and vampires, then I would never, ever have even entertained it.

But it was real. I knew it was real. It made sense somehow, the jumbled pieces of my person somehow starting to straighten. Pieces I had always known weren't in the right place, but wasn't sure why.

"Francis, when I lost my parents, I knew something bigger than just a car crash or some accident had happened. I *knew* it. Nobody believed me, and even I wrote it off as grief. But I was right all along. They did actually vanish, into a place I couldn't reach. And now, for the first time in as long as I can remember, I might have an actual reason why."

"Give me that hip-flask," Francis said after a pause, reaching for the silver flask she had insisted we bring outside with us. I passed it to her, and she took a long swig. "Want some?"

"What is it?"

"Brandy."

"No, thanks. Francis, what I don't understand is, why did they never tell me? About magic or angels or any of this? Surely that's a thing you tell your kid? That you're an *angel*." I tried to keep the rising accusation from my voice, to suppress the twang of betrayal threatening to bubble up and spill over.

I had never truly connected with my mom, but my dad... He had been my best friend my whole life. We shared everything. I couldn't believe he would omit something like this.

"Maybe they did, and magic made you forget? Hell, maybe they don't know? There could be a hundred reasons." Her demeanor shifted from disbelieving to all-knowing as she peered at me. "When magic is involved, anything goes," she said, in her most assured tone.

"A second ago you thought I hit my head," I said.

"Well, now I've had a few moments to think, and a tot of brandy, I figure if Mr. Nox can be an angel, why can't you?"

"That's not really how I'm coming at it," I said doubtfully.

She shrugged. "You've always known there was something funny about your parents going missing. This makes sense. They would have been able to enter the magic world, this Veil place, is that right?"

I nodded. "And if they really are angels, they're most likely still alive. Angels don't die." My throat tightened as I said the word *die*.

For the first time in a long while, I was actually allowing myself the slightest gleam of hope that they still lived. The family I had already grieved for.

I saw the doubt in Francis' warm face, and voiced what we were both thinking. "But why haven't they come back to me if they're alive? Or sent me a message?"

"Maybe they're being held captive? Or magic made them forget about you?"

"Maybe," I said, dropping my gaze to the bright grass beneath my feet. "Maybe." I looked back at Francis, who was gulping more brandy. "This is a whole shitload of maybes."

"True. But a shitload of maybe is a whole lot more than you've ever had before," she said as she patted my hand.

I blinked as my eyes grew hot. She was right. "Oh,

sweetie," she smiled, and pulled me into a hug. "You can cry, if you need to. This is a lot."

I hugged her back, hard. "Thank you, Francis. You're good to me."

"Honey, you're the best thing that happened to me since coming to live in this damn home. Especially since you started sleeping with hot magic men."

She grinned at me as I pulled back from her, wiping a few escaped tears from my cheeks.

"I wonder what magic they have? They should be able to tell you, when you find them."

When you find them. The words ricocheted around in my head.

"I have to help Nox lift his curse first. Then we're going to find them. He's going to help me."

The problem was, though, I had no idea how long it would take to find the sins, the pages, and the book.

Trying to find out what had happened to my parents had been important before, but now that there was a good chance they were still alive - it was more than important.

What if Francis was right and they were being held captive? *Something* was stopping them from contacting me - what if they were in danger?

"If anyone can help you, it's him," Francis said. "He's a good one to have on your side."

"Yes. He is." Thoughts of Nox and magic and power swilled about in my brain.

"There is one more thing," I said. I'd been concentrating so hard on my mom and dad that the rest of what the genie had said had taken a back seat.

"What's that?"

"If I, erm, sleep with Nox again, I'll get more of his power, but it won't kill me."

Francis' face lit up. "Well that is good news," she beamed.

"No, it's not. It'll weaken him until he is as good as the angel version of dead."

"Oh." Her face fell. "So, you're like his kryptonite?"

I gave her a look. "You've been watching superhero movies?"

"Superman was made before you were born," she said, shaking her head at me. "Well ain't that a shitter. You meet each other, have epic sex, then find out that sex can kill one of you."

"Yeah."

"Sure you don't want some of this?" She offered me the hip flask again.

"I'm sure. Thanks."

She nodded. "Yeah, you're probably right. You've got a lot to do, what with lifting a curse on the devil, finding your family, and not having sex with the hottest guy on Earth. Brandy might not help."

I stared at her a moment and then held out my hand. "Give me the flask."

TWENTY-NINE

BETH

L ifting Nox's curse was the most important thing to focus on. This new information about my parents didn't change that, much as a part of me wished it did.

He was in charge, both in a professional sense, and in every other sense. I had nothing compared to him, no contacts, no money, no information. And even if you removed the constant fighting against our desire for each other, there was a massive urgency to finding the lost sins. Somebody was trying to frame him for Alex's murder, hellhounds were escaping, and we'd missed the Sloth page by only a week.

When you stacked up what needed the most urgent attention, there was no denying that my missing mom and dad were near the bottom of the pile. Whatever had kept them away from me for five years was unlikely to change in the next couple weeks.

. . .

"Good afternoon, Beth."

A deep male voice startled me, and I looked up from our park bench to see a man standing before us.

Not a man, I corrected myself, taking in his long golden hair, square jaw and surfer-style linen shirt. An angel.

"Gabriel," I said, standing up quickly. "What are you-"

He cut me off. "I'm sorry for coming unannounced. I stole a moment, and now must take advantage of it. I want you to listen to me, please."

"I'll listen to you, honey," said Francis. "All day, every day. Damn, you're a fine looking man."

I threw her a look. "Francis, this is the angel Gabriel."

Francis gaped between me and Gabriel, and he gave her a small smile before turning his attention back to me.

"Lucifer must regain his power."

I thrust my chin out. "Why don't you take a turn with it, if it's that important to you?"

"I am not designed to withstand such magic. He was created for this role, and the world needs him. Not just your world. Ours, too." Nox had said the same thing about him being the only person who could handle the power of the devil, so I didn't question that. But the rest...

"What do you mean, the world needs him? Are you talking about there being more sinners since he gave up his power?"

"There is more to it than that. It is true that whilst the sinners have nothing to fear they grow in number. But the balance of magic is shifting, and the gods have felt it."

"The gods?"

"Yes. Michael does not want to believe it, but I suspect Examinus is telling the truth about a war coming. And Lucifer will be the first target of Examinus' enemies. He is his strongest weapon, and they will wish him out of the game early. Without his full strength, the other gods could kill him."

My stomach knotted at his words, a heavy feeling gripping my chest at the thought of losing Nox.

"Which other gods? Gods you work for?"

"Examinus' enemies are not gods I hold allegiance with."

"Why didn't you say any of this to Nox before, at the casino?"

"Lucifer already knows that if there is a war between the gods, he will die if he is not at full strength. And he knows somebody out there is working to see him powerless. Michael told him that war is not coming, and I am not inclined to disagree with him publicly."

"Then why tell me? Surely that's the same thing?"

"No, I don't think it is. You clearly mean something to Lucifer. Something I have not seen before with him." Interest shimmered in his bright blue eyes. "Don't tell him I visited you. Don't even tell him that I believe the war to be real - he already knows. He knew the day a hellhound sought him out in London."

"Then what do you want me to do?"

"Help him return to power, for the sake of his own life."

"That's why you're here? You care about his life?"

"He is my brother."

That wasn't a real answer. I scowled at the angel, utterly unsure whether to trust him. Nox definitely didn't, and that meant more to me than any of Gabriel's words.

"You don't need to trust me right away," Gabriel said, correctly reading my expression. "But when the time comes, help him." He stepped forward and held out his hand. There was something small and gold in it. "If you need me, or if I can help him, use this."

I cautiously held out my own hand and he dropped the item into my palm. It was a tiny turtle. I looked down at it, and when I looked back up, he was gone.

Francis let out a long whistle. "So, all angels are hot as hell, I see. Not just your Mr. Nox."

"Yeah," I muttered, studying the gold turtle. It looked like a tourist trinket from a beach hawker or something.

Did Gabriel really want to help his brother? Or was this a trick, something to further reduce Nox's power and clear the way for whatever god wanted to fight with Examinus?

The thought of Nox being dragged into a war with beings as powerful as gods made me angry on his behalf. Fighting for a cause you believed in, or for a true loyalty, was one thing. But fighting as a weapon for a being you despised was shit.

And if he didn't have his power back.... He may not even get the chance to fight at all.

THIRTY

BETH

"Francis, it's time for everyone to come in now," called a singsong voice. A young orderly headed our way, her hair pulled into a neat bun and a cheerful smile on her face that couldn't have been further from the bleak expression on my own.

Francis waved. "That's Lina. That means my dinner is ready. I got an appetite, now I seen that hunk of an angel." She heaved her large frame up off the wooden bench but paused. Her eyes narrowed. "You feel that?"

"Feel what?"

"Hot breeze. The kind you don't get in England." She looked around herself, and a wave of hot air buffed against my bare arms. A faint smell of sulphur carried to my nose, and my hairs stood on end.

"Francis, I think this might be magic. We need to get back to the home." I moved toward her fast, intending to hurry her along, but a clap of thunder made me slow, casting my eyes upward.

"What is that god-awful smell?" asked the orderly as she reached us, looping an arm through Francis' and steering her toward the main building of Lavender Oaks. "And there wasn't any rain forecast." She looked up at the clouds moving over us.

I didn't want to answer her, but I recognized the smell. "I really, really hope I'm wrong, but I think it might be a hellhound."

Lina's pretty face screwed up in confusion. "A what?"

I grabbed Francis' other arm and began to walk, as fast as she could keep up.

But we were too late.

As I glanced over my shoulder there was a shuddering crack, and the ground beneath our feet heaved.

All of us stumbled, Lina managing to hang on to Francis. I was thrown backward, spinning and dropping hard to one knee before regaining my footing. A massive rent in the well-kept lawn was growing before me, and the stench of sulphur poured from it on stifling air.

"Beth!" Francis yelled. "Where is that angel of yours?"

I'd asked 'that angel of mine' for space. And he'd been gracious enough to give it to me.

Oh shit, shit, shit. I scrambled backward as something that looked a lot like fire flickered inside the hole in the ground.

The hellhound sprang up out of the crevice in the blink of an eye, the ground shuddering as its huge paws connected. It swung its massive maw, sniffing the air.

Lina screamed, and I might well have done too, if it weren't for the very, very strange feeling welling up in my chest.

The beast was as huge as the last one, monstrous and flaming. Its red eyes fixed on me as its shoulders dropped low and its front paws clawed at the ground.

It was getting ready to pounce.

But so was something inside *me*.

All the anger and frustration and downright over-whelming confusion seemed be coming together in a mass of something that burned under my ribs. It was hot and fierce, and I knew that it wasn't a part of me. My emotions were feeding it, for sure, but the power wasn't mine. It was Nox's.

I could sense the creature's desire for the fight, his hunger for the taste of my flesh.

"Run!" I bellowed at Lina and Francis. They were the other side of the enormous dog, so I didn't see if they heeded my instruction. But I sure did.

I whirled, racing for the small copse of trees thirty feet away.

If it weren't for my head-start on the dog, I wouldn't have made it. But I did, leaping for the lowest branch as I felt the wave of unnatural heat smash into my back.

I missed. My jump carried me too far forward, and not high enough, and I crashed into the thick bark of the tree before bouncing off to the side.

An awful bark sounded from the dog, so loud that the pain in my ears and head was worse than that of tumbling to the pine-covered earth.

A flaming paw swiped at me, and I barely pushed myself out of its way in time.

"Stop!"

A female voice bellowed the command, and I found myself freezing for a split second, before the realization that the hellhound had stopped moving hit me.

"Up the fucking tree, Beth. Now."

I scrambled to my feet and the owner of the familiar voice came into view.

"Rory," I gasped, scraping my fingers on the rough trunk as I tried to get enough purchase to climb. Adrenaline made my muscles stronger and numbed the pain.

The hound snarled and turned to face her. I dragged myself a few feet up the tree, trying to get higher, survival instinct pushing me on.

"You shouldn't be here, you naughty hound," she called to the beast. It barked again, and I winced. I reached a sturdy branch, and felt a modicum of relief as I managed to get my feet onto it, ensuring my whole body was at least ten feet above the ground. Although I was pretty sure the hellhound could jump that high.

I sucked in air as I stared down at Rory and the hellhound. She was wearing a high-waisted black pencil-skirt with a skin-tight scarlet shirt, and she looked like she should be bossing some entrepreneur Instagram account somewhere, not facing off a monster from hell.

I thought I couldn't be more in awe of her, until the thing pounced. She threw up both her hands and a shimmering wave of pink energy blasted from her palms. The hellhound yelped as the pink magic hit it square on, and it flew backward, slamming down onto its back. Pawing at its face, it rolled back onto its feet.

Rory didn't budge. The pixie may have an attitude problem, but she was fierce as hell.

The smell worsened, and I wondered if I should climb higher. "Can you kill it?" I called to her.

"Nobody can kill it. And I can't send it back to hell, either." Her clipped voice was tight, her focus entirely on the dog as it began to prowl up and down in front of her. Flames licked higher from its sleek body.

"What can I do?"

"Stay the fuck out of the way until Nox gets here."

At the mention of Nox, the flames covering the hellhound seemed to turn a deeper red, and it turned its head to my tree. Those scarlet, feral eyes found me, and the alien feeling pulsed in my chest. It was anger, bordering on rage, at my own impotence, at my inability to cope with the situations I kept finding myself in.

The hellhound turned, approaching the tree.

The thing could sense Nox's power in me, I realized.

Rory swore. "That's the fucking opposite of what I just told you to do!"

"I'm not doing it on purpose!"

The hellhound laid one giant paw on the trunk of the tree, and my heart thudded against my ribs as I saw what was going to happen. Fire sparked against the bark, tiny at first, then growing as it snaked up the trunk.

"Shit." My tree was on fire. I had two choices; jump or climb higher. Neither were appealing and both could easily end in my death. "How long do trees take to burn down?" I yelled, as I looked up to the top of the tree.

"Longer than it takes hellhounds to rip you apart," Rory yelled back.

As I suspected, my choice was up. I reached high for the branch above me and started to scramble.

The branches got less sturdy as I got higher, and the foliage got denser, blocking my view of pretty much everything except the wood around me. I was sweating, adrenaline the only thing keeping my muscles moving and my hands steady as I pushed on higher.

Abruptly my head cleared the mass of green leaves around me, and I registered that I had reached the top. I gripped the diminishing trunk hard and looked around myself.

I must have been fifty feet up, and I could see the dark hole in the ground that the hound had come up through, but there was no sign of the creature.

Praying that didn't mean he'd begun to climb the tree, I took a few deep breaths.

The smell of sulphur washed over me, and a blast of heat was the only warning I got before pain ripped through my foot.

I cried out, throwing myself to the side. Pure panic filled me. I had nowhere to go. Pain made my vision blur and heat was stifling my thoughts.

Fire blasted into my vision as I looked down, seeing the hellhound pushing up through the thick leaves, all of which were catching aflame around it's huge head. He snapped again at my feet and my movement was instinctive. I avoided his snarling jaws, but I lost my grip on the top of the tree. I slipped, and the world moved into slow motion as I realized I was going to fall.

Straight into the creature's jaws.

Fear, as much as strength, forced my body to push against the wood, launching myself away from the hell-hound. Branches scratched my arms as I began to plummet, head first toward the ground. Better the ground than the fire, I thought, all rational thought fleeing me as I squeezed my eyes shut.

Something slammed into me, knocking all the breath from my body. My eyes flew open as I choked, unable to process anything. Had I hit the ground?

No. I was moving. Gold filled my blurred vision, and I tried to suck in air, my lungs burning.

"You're okay, just winded. Hold on."

"Nox," I tried to say, but I couldn't speak. I didn't have enough air. My head spun, thoughts swimming in and out of focus as air streamed over us.

He had caught me. I was falling to my death and he caught me. A real-life guardian angel.

"Breathe, Beth. You're okay."

Relief filled me as much as the oxygen did as my chest began to move.

"I have to set you down. Don't move, I'll be right back."

My eyes still weren't working properly, dizziness

warping everything as I felt ground beneath my backside. "Nox," I choked out, as he let go of me.

"I have to send the hound back to hell. I'll be right back." I got a glimpse of his face as my vision began to clear, then a blur of gold as he launched himself off the ground, back into the air.

I collapsed onto my back, drawing in as much air as I could. I was on grass, and there were trees around me that weren't on fire, but I had no idea where I was. And I couldn't care less.

I'd truly believed I was going to die.

Again.

Just weeks ago, I'd felt the same impending doom, the same sense of resigned terror, when I had been under the surface of the river Thames.

Nox claimed that he didn't rescue me from Max, that I'd rescued myself. But he'd sure as hell rescued me this time.

I sat up, adrenaline coursing through me, my limbs beginning to shake as my breathing steadied.

He'd saved my life, catching me as I fell through the sky like a freaking superhero.

In that moment, I knew that whatever Nox became when his full power returned, it didn't matter. Whatever he was to the rest of the world meant nothing.

To me, he was a hero. My hero.

～

As soon as I saw him flying through the blue sky toward me I got to my feet. He was shirtless, the black of his jeans and the gold of his wings ethereally beautiful. He landed before me, power radiating from him. "I'm sorry. I'm sorry I was almost too late."

"You were right on time," I said, moving to him. "You saved my life."

"I will destroy any who threaten it again."

I believed him. His eyes were granite hard, and emotion twisted his face into fury as he spoke. "Kiss me."

"Beth-" I stepped into him, heat rushing my body. I held my hand up, pressing fingers over his mouth to stop him speaking.

"Nox, you just saved my life. I was certain I would die. I need you to kiss me."

Passion filled his eyes, but it wasn't the sultry lust I was used to from him. It was deeper. It was *need*. The same need I felt for him.

I dropped my hand and his lips met mine. His hand found the back of my head, and I pressed my palms against his chest and lost myself to his passion.

I poured my gratitude, my respect, my awe for him into the kiss and prayed it got through to him, because I didn't yet know how to say it out loud.

Something was shifting between us, and I didn't know if it was because there was a part of him inside me, or if it was just the bond between us growing.

Whatever it was, it was dangerous. It could consume me, I was sure.

"Beth," he breathed against my lips, and I waited for

the rest of the sentence, but there was nothing. He was just saying my name.

"Thank you. For saving me."

"I will save you in a hundred fucking ways, for the rest of your life."

THIRTY-ONE

NOX

Her nails dug into my chest at my words, and she leaned back, her big eyes finding and focusing on mine.

"The rest of my life?" she whispered.

I ground my teeth. I had never needed anything as much as I needed her. She was a drug, intoxicating.

"As long as you let me. And possibly longer."

A smile flitted over her face, before worry dominated it. "Nox, Gabriel came."

"What?"

"Gabriel came to see me. He thinks the war is real, and that his brother is wrong."

Fury made every muscle in my body tense, and when Beth's hands flinched on my skin I realized I was pulsing heat. "Why did he come to see you instead of me?"

"He hoped I could convince you to get your power back. He says he cares about your life, and that it is in danger."

I dropped my head to her, our foreheads touching. A heavy resignation was taking hold of me. I would not let asshole angels or fucked-up gods ruin Beth's life.

"We will do everything we can to find the sins and the book. I will join you in that office every day, and set ten more people to the task. This will end, and it will end soon."

She moved to look at me, her face still creased with worry. "What if we can't find everything?"

"Then we finish this without my full power," I said.

"Finish this?" she said doubtfully. "As in, go to war for a god you hate? Without your proper strength?"

"I'm powerful without all the sins," I told her. And I was. But not powerful enough to go up against a god. Whomever Examinus had fallen out with was trying to take me out before I got my power restored for a good fucking reason. But Beth didn't need to know that. Not yet, anyway.

"Okay. But we should hit this hard. Do nothing but work on this."

"I agree. Just as soon as you've had some rest." I watched her face as she thought about arguing, and changed her mind.

"Rory was amazing. I definitely want her to teach me how to look after myself."

"Well, it appears she doesn't need to teach you how to climb a tree."

Beth laughed, and the sound made me positive; I'd throw myself of a cliff for her, wings or none. "No.

Apparently a flaming hell-beast gives you the impetus to do that by yourself."

"You know, I'm one of those flaming hell-beasts."

"Yeah, but you look really fucking good in a suit," she grinned at me.

"I love it when you swear." My voice was a growl, and desire filled her laughing eyes.

"I know. That's why I did it."

I pulled her close, kissing her deeply. My cock strained in my trousers, my need for her making my heart pound in my chest. She must have been able to feel it. I hoped she could.

"I want you. So much. I can't believe I could hurt you by showing you how much I..." She trailed off, her lips still brushing mine. Had she been about to say love you?

"Show me," I said, unable to stop myself. "Show me how much you want me. I need to feel it. I don't care what it does to me."

"Of course you do."

"No. I don't. We'll get my power back soon, and then it won't matter. I need you."

"No. I won't hurt you."

"And I won't go without you. You make me stronger, Beth. Fuck what that asshole genie says. When I'm inside you, when I'm so fucking deep we may as well be one person..."

She moaned against my mouth, pressing herself tighter to my body. "You make me something new, Beth. I need you."

THIRTY-TWO

BETH

Nox's words rolled around in my head, echoing over the swells of pleasure taking over my body as he dropped his head and planted his hot lips against my neck.

Could we risk it? Could he handle more loss of power? His hand pushed into my hair, fingers closing and pulling my head back, exposing my throat.

Nerve endings fired all over my body, my chest heaving as he kissed his way down to the neckline of my shirt.

"Nox," I panted. He straightened, the feral look in his eyes setting fresh waves of need pulsing through my blood. "Nox, I don't even know where we are."

He glanced around us. "Regent's Park," he growled. He scooped me up and I yelped in surprise. "Listen to me, Beth," he said, as he strode toward a copse of dense trees. "I'm going to create a forcefield around us, and I swear to you that nobody will see or hear us. And you are going to scream my name. You are going to feel every-thing I do to you. Because this is the only time we are doing it. You are going to behave like we only have these few hours together, for the rest of time." He tilted me, and looked directly into my eyes. His were blazing with light, and memories of the night we spent together rushed me, making my already throbbing sex heat further. "You are going to throw every fucking inhibition you have out completely. You will give yourself to me, utterly. Do you understand?"

I bit down on my lip and nodded at him.

Words had fled.

I couldn't say no to him now, if my life depended on it. I would give up anything to have him claim me, to feel that exquisite bliss only he could instill.

"Say it. Out loud."

"I understand."

"Tell me you're going to give yourself to me. Completely."

He had stopped under a massive oak tree. The same weird bubble that had been present in the casino with his brothers flared to life around us, but I barely noticed it.

There was an edge to his voice. He'd been barely able to keep control last time, barely able to keep himself from what he had been denied for so long.

But this possessiveness was new. And hot as hell.

I wanted nothing more than this god of a man, this angel, to want to own me. No part of me railed against the idea of a man claiming my body, as I might expect it to. Nox was bound to me, and I to him, there was no question that he could have me. I was his.

My pulse raced as we stared at each other.

We both knew this was more than sex. He felt as I did, he felt the bond, I could see it in his every glance, his every flinch, his constant need.

"I'm yours, Nox."

He moved in an instant. With barely time to take a breath, he crushed the air out of me as he slammed me against the tree trunk behind me.

His hands gripped my ribs, then slid up my body as his lips devoured my neck, my jaw, then found my mouth.

Like a man possessed, he kissed me. The power of Lust blasted through me, and for a surreal moment, I could feel him in a way that was not physical.

His soul. Dark and fierce and so full of passion it bordered on untamable. And I was at its core. Every ounce of that wild, flaming, passionate energy revolved around his perception of me.

Elation coursed through me, and I kissed him back harder, pouring my own emotion into the embrace, unable to magically bare my soul to him but desperate for him to know I felt the same.

He grunted as I snagged his bottom lip between my teeth, and then he moved back to grab the hem of my shirt and lift.

I leaned back against the tree trunk, panting, as he slowly drew it up my torso, taking me in, eyes alive with want. When his hands brushed over the sides of my chest, I lifted my arms above my head. My shirt reached my wrists, and instead of pulling it off, he closed his fist around my hands, pinning me.

His other hand stroked down my naked stomach, deftly unsnapping my jeans when he reached the waistband.

"Nox," I breathed. "I can't move."

"You don't need to move. You need to stay still while I make you forget your own fucking name."

Delicious anticipation shuddered through me as he eased my jeans down over my right hip, then my left.

He hissed in a breath, then pressed himself against me, tilting my chin up to look into his face. My own flamed with need.

"I am going to use magic to keep your hands where I want them." It wasn't a request for permission, but he paused long enough to note no objection from me.

When he dropped his hand from my wrists, I felt no change in pressure. I tugged experimentally, and a little fizz emanated down my arms. My nipples hardened.

A wicked gleam of hunger lit Nox's face, and he dropped to his knees.

The sight of him before me, shirtless, golden wings spread, and on his knees, elicited an actual moan from my lips.

He tugged my jeans all the way down, stopping at my booted feet. Slowly, he separated my thighs, until my jeans stretched between my ankles.

He hooked one finger into the side of my panties, and tracked it all the way down. He hesitated when he reached the hot wetness there, a rumbling sounding from his chest as his eyes flicked to my face, then back to my underwear.

He moved his finger back up, pulled the fabric to one side, and leaned forward. I felt his hot breath whisper over me, and tried to buck my hips forward to meet his mouth. But his other hand flattened against my belly, keeping me still.

"I told you to stay still. This will not be over quickly, Beth. We get one forbidden moment. And I am going to make you wish every fucking second was an hour."

I felt his words on my sex, he was so close to me. I writhed, and the hand on my tummy moved round to my ass. Slowly, his fingers moved behind me, under me. When I felt them brush the aching wetness, I gasped.

His right hand still holding my panties to the side, he flicked his tongue out, brushing so close to where I wanted him. My legs moved, opening wider for him, the jeans pulling at my ankles.

His head moved, and when his tongue darted out again, he hit my clit directly. I pushed against him and cried out as his finger dipped into me.

"Nox. Please."

His tongue worked over me, heat rushing my core and my muscles clenching around his fingers.

"I want you, Nox, please." I was going to come if he kept doing what he was doing. "I want you inside me when I come." The words came ragged from my throat, and they were met with a growl that caused heavenly vibrations to ripple through me. I squirmed against him, closing my eyes.

"Look at me." The command was forceful, and my eyes fluttered open as I felt him press into me, two fingers now. The pleasure radiating out from my center was tightening, knotting, building. I knew what that meant.

I needed him inside me, needed to come around him. And I knew what would make him stop teasing me.

"Nox, take me. Take me right now. Claim me as yours."

His fingers stilled. "You're not going to make me stop," he hissed.

"Own me. Own me in the deepest way you can. Make me come around you."

I saw the control break in his eyes. I felt it snap in the bond between us.

In a rush, his hands left my body, and he was turning me, pressing my chest against the tree, one hand wrapped around my waist and the other around my raised wrists.

I pushed my ass back against him, the bark of the tree scratching against my chest and sending new sensations lancing through me.

"Own me. I'm yours. Take what's yours."

His hand left my wrist long enough to unfasten his own jeans, and my panties were pulled aside again. When I felt his hot, hard head pressed against me, I thought I might come then and there.

His lips found my ear, and his arm squeezed hard around my middle. "You're fucking divine, Beth."

He pushed, his swollen cock entering my wetness. I

forced myself not to tighten around him, and I felt a hand on my jaw, pulling my head back. Hot lips pressed against my neck as he pushed further into me, filling me. Claiming me.

Only when he couldn't be any deeper inside me did I let my muscles clench against him. We moaned together, his grip on my throat tightening, and he thrust hard.

My moan turned into a cry, and he growled as he buried his face in my hair, pulling my body so tight against his that his searing flesh burned against my own.

He thrust again, harder, and the knot that had been building inside me sharpened, my awareness narrowing to nothing but him inside me.

"I'm going to come," I gasped.

He powered into me, making me aware of parts of my own body I had never known even existed. Lights danced in front of my eyes as they closed. "I own you, Beth. Every inch of your gorgeous fucking body is mine. Come for me."

I let go, pleasure exploding through me.

He didn't slow, didn't speed up, just kept that exquisite length moving in and out me, pressing me hard to his solid body, holding me together and wave after wave of bliss rocked through me.

"Nox."

"Mine."

"Nox."

He pulled out, and I whimpered in protest and my eyes opened. The power holding my arms up vanished at the same time he spun me around. They fell, still bound by my t-shirt, over his shoulders.

Primal, wicked light danced in his eyes as he lifted me, careful when he pressed my back against the rough tree when I was high enough to guide himself back between my legs.

"Yes." I pulled my arms tight around his neck as he cupped my ass and pushed hard into me. He rocked so that my clit rubbed against him, and his mouth closed over mine, swallowing my gasp.

He stayed deep, the long thrusts making way for a rocking movement that set my whole pelvis on fire.

The whole world fell away once more as I ground myself against him.

"Never this good." I got snippets of his words between his frenzied kisses, his accent thick and his tone primal.

"Again," I gasped, unable to form more words to let him know I was close.

He rocked harder, filling me utterly, and I felt him jerk and swell inside me. The knowledge that he was filling me with his come overtook me, and my own orgasm tore through me. He roared as he felt me around him, letting himself go completely, crushing me to him.

I gasped for breath, dizzy.

"Mine."

"Yours."

THIRTY-THREE

BETH

"Morning, beautiful."

I rolled over, blinking sleep from my eyes. Nox gazed down at me, his eyes utterly void of any sign of sleep.

"Hi." The smell of coffee filtered through to me as I let myself take in Nox's bare chest.

The memories of the previous night slowly infiltrated my sleep haze, and I sat up straight.

The park. We had done exactly what were supposed to be avoiding.

After Nox flew us home, laid me in his bed and wrapped his warm body around mine, I'd all but passed out.

But now, in the light of morning, reality settled in. *Sex with Nox weakened him.*

"Are you okay?" I asked him.

"Better than okay. I'm with you."

Warmth flooded my chest, but it didn't expel the

concern. "Do I... Are my wings any more solid?" I half screwed my face up as his eyes flicked over my shoulders.

"Yes. A little. They suit you." There was no worry in his face. No pain or fear. Just his usual gorgeous self-assured gleam.

"And your power? It's okay?"

He handed me a coffee cup. "We have a lot to do today. I am going to come with you to see Malcolm and introduce the new researchers. Finding the book should be our number one priority."

"That's not an answer, Nox."

"My power will be restored when we lift my curse. We do not need to worry about it now."

Knots formed in my stomach. "You can feel it, can't you. The loss of your power." It wasn't a question. I *had* weakened him.

"Loss of power is nothing compared to what I gain from being with you."

"You're just saying that to make me feel better."

"I'm saying it because it is true. There is a new strength building inside me, Beth. And for a being as old as me, new is a very, very valuable thing."

He smiled, then leaned in to kiss me softly.

"Now, you're going to have to get dressed, before you make me lose some more power." His tone was both teasing and sultry, and I forced myself to relax. He didn't regret what we had done. That was clear. And I sure as hell didn't regret it.

"Okay. But you're going to have to give me at least twenty minutes in your shower first. I love your shower."

"Only if I can watch."

"Pervert."

"You have no idea."

Malc did not look particularly impressed when Nox told him ten new researchers would be assigned to looking for the sins.

"But Boss, I don't have time to manage that many people. I'm working through all the footage with Max in for three weeks prior to the theft of the book, and looking for Envy. And Beth is working through any transaction that could be the sale of something paper."

"Have half the researchers help Beth with those transactions, and have the other half working on everything we knew about Envy before we lost him. They already know the software, they won't need much of your time. Just answer questions when they have them. You stay with the footage of Max. He must have met whoever hired him in person at least once, and there's cameras all over London."

We left Malc's darkroom, his wall of screens filled with the faces of his new, temporary team, and entered my office next door.

"I have to talk with Rory," Nox said, touching my arm to turn me to him.

"I want to see Rory too," I said. "I didn't get a chance to thank her."

"I'll pass it on. You'll be okay here?"

"Of course I will. I've got shit to do."

"Good. I'll be back in an hour, then I'll help." Nox kissed me on the cheek, sparks of heat simmering into my skin at the contact.

My hand flew up, stopping his retreat, and I turned his face, his stubble rough under my fingertips. My lips closed over his, and I channeled my emotion into them.

"See you soon."

I'd been at my laptop for about half an hour when the door flew open.

"Rory?"

She looked furious, her resting-bitch-face amplified by a hundred, and I gripped the arm of my chair as I turned to her.

"They've arrested him."

"What?"

"The Ward have arrested Nox. For Alex's murder."

I was on my feet before I'd even digested her words. "But he can't have-"

She carried on over me. "Banks has taken him for questioning. If they find enough evidence, he'll be taken off-world for a trial."

"Taken off-world?" A surge of fierce protectiveness that I had never felt before in my life flooded my body, and my fists clenched. "They're not taking him anywhere." Even if I couldn't stop them, Nox wouldn't allow it.

Rory shook her head. Real concern filled her usually cold eyes. "The Ward is powerful, Beth. If they take him, we can't do anything about it, nor can he."

"Shit. He's been framed. He didn't do it."

"I know that," she spat. "But unless we can prove it, that means fucking nothing. They told him they found one of his feathers at the scene, that's as good as a damned confession to them."

My mind raced, and mercifully it didn't fill with blind panic. If Nox couldn't do anything, I had to.

"Whoever set him up is the same person who paid Max," I said, thinking aloud. "It has to be, with the feather and everything. That's a message."

"So?"

"So, Alex was probably killed for no reason other than to get Nox arrested. That's the motive." A stabbing guilt punctured my gut at the affirmation. Alex was killed because of me. Not because he'd stolen the wrong thing or pissed off the wrong person. He was killed to make it look like the guy I was now sleeping with had got jealous and committed murder.

"What's your point?"

"My point is that if you remove the motive, you're left with the murder weapon and the opportunity to solve. That's what it always is on the TV - means, motive, and opportunity. Rory, we have to find out who the real murderer is. There's no other way to help Nox."

Her lips tightened a moment, then she nodded.

"Fine. How?"

"Well, we can ignore motive. And we know the weapon was magic, or teeth. And that there was a powerful magical signature." I rubbed my sweating hands together, thinking. "We need to go back to the scene, see if there's anything there that can help us." I couldn't think of anything else to do.

"The Ward already went over that place."

"Yeah, but they were looking for evidence that it was Nox. We might be able to find something they didn't." I was clutching at straws, I knew. I'd been there myself, and had seen nothing but mess and blood. And I couldn't even sense magic. "Rory, can you sense other's magic?"

"Of course I can. How do think I knew you were being attacked by a hellhound?"

"Oh, yeah. Erm, thanks for that, by the way."

She shrugged. "I was on babysitting duty."

"Really?"

"Yes. Sitting in a car round the corner while you get pissed with your ancient friend. Exactly how I planned to spend my career." She rolled her eyes.

"My ancient friend is worth getting pissed with. You should try it someday," I snapped, immediately defensive of Francis.

"I wish I could." Rory gave me a sarcastic smile, and I felt a little bad. Francis wouldn't be able to see her. Hardly anybody could see her.

"We should get to Alex's," I said, reaching for my jacket.

"I'll call Claude."

THIRTY-FOUR

BETH

Arriving at Alex's didn't feel good. The tower block was dark and foreboding, and nothing about the district felt safe. Not that I felt unsafe with Rory at my side. I'd seen what she could do.

"This is a shithole." Rory's lip curled as we made our way up the concrete fire escape. Litter was everywhere, and the distinct smell of urine invaded my nostrils.

"Yeah."

When we reached the door to Alex's place, Rory pushed past me and held her hand over the knob. After a couple seconds, I heard the lock click. We carefully moved the police tape that marked it as a place we should not enter and entered.

The blood stain was still there. It was clearly never coming out. But the nausea I felt last time was absent, replaced by hard focus. Nox was depending on us. On me.

Part of me didn't fully believe that. He was the damn devil; he oozed power. If he didn't want to stay somewhere, I struggled to believe anyone could keep him contained. But two things worried me enough that a tight urgency had taken over that disbelief. Rory's evident concern, and the fact that only that night, *I had made him weaker.*

"This is even more of a shithole than the outside," Rory muttered. The lights in the apartment were off and the drapes drawn, and a dank, dusty haze fell over the piles of mess. She picked up one of the jewelry boxes on the kitchen counter and opened it, peering inside. "This is a terrible reproduction of Tiffany," she announced. I wasn't surprised.

"Can you sense any magic?"

She shook her head. "No. And I can't sense Nox either."

"Then look for anything that might give us a clue. Something that could have been left here by a wolf, or Nox's brothers."

"Those are your suspects?"

"And Wrath. I can't think of anyone else who would want to frame Nox. Can you?"

"Beth, he's pissed off half the population of the Veil over the last few hundred years."

"Oh. Then look for signs of them, too," I said sarcastically. She rolled her eyes, and turned back to scanning the piles of junk in the gloom.

I moved into the bedroom, feeling a tiny pang at seeing a sweater I used to wear all the time when Alex and I had lived together. It seemed like a lifetime ago.

My gaze fell on the robe dangling off the edge of the bed. It was a white robe, with faint stains up the side, and it sparked a memory. Slowly, I reached out and lifted it up, holding as little of the fabric in my fingers as I could to shake it out. There was a small embroidered logo on the front.

My pulse quickened as I read the words aloud "Scared Sleep Spa".

Shit.

Alex had got in over his head, after all.

"Rory! Rory, I think Alex stole Sloth's page!"

She sauntered over to me and I waved the robe at her. "This robe, it's from Sloth's spa. The page was stolen a week ago, and Alex is—was—apparently a thief for hire." I gestured at the piles of gear all over the apartment, my voice hitching with excitement. "It makes perfect sense."

If I was right, then we actually had something to go on. And even better, finding Alex's killer might lead us to Sloth's page.

The pixie regarded me a moment, then nodded. "Okay. Now what?"

"We look for the page? It might still be here?"

Doubt covered her pretty face. "Whoever killed him will have taken the page, I'm sure."

"True." I scowled. Maybe it wasn't as good a lead as I thought it was. We still only had the motive, though that had changed from 'frame Nox for murder', to 'steal

Sloth's page'. "Do you think the person who hired Alex to steal the page killed him so he wouldn't tell anyone? Or maybe Alex tried to charge them more money or something, and they got angry?"

Rory's eyes narrowed in thought. "Maybe. Or maybe someone else found out he had the page, and wanted it themselves. Should we go and see Sloth?"

My lips curled back from my teeth involuntarily at the thought of going back to that place. "Not if we don't have to."

"We could visit from a distance?"

I looked at her, raising my eyebrows in question. "What do you mean?"

"There must be cameras around the spa. We could get Malc to get the footage up. See if we can find Alex in the area, and see if he meets with anyone, or had an accomplice."

"Yes. Great idea."

If I had to set foot inside that foul place again, then I would, for Nox. But I'd try everything else I could first.

"Are you sure the boss won't mind me changing projects?" Malc said, giving Rory a sideways glance. She seemed not to care about the 'don't get too close to a vampire' rule, and was standing directly behind him. I was keeping my distance, sitting near to the dark office's only door.

"The boss is currently being held for questioning for

a murder he didn't commit. I'm going to go out on a limb and assume clearing his name by finding the real killer will trump his other priorities."

Her voice was characteristically dripping with venom, and Malc threw me a look before his fingers began to fly over his keyboard.

"As you wish, your liege," he said. "I already downloaded footage of the CCTV around the spa. There's nothing covering the entrance though, and footfall in that part of town is high, so I had nothing to go on. If we're looking for a specific person on a specific date though - that I can work with."

A picture of Alex, almost definitely a police mugshot, popped up on the screens on the wall before us. "This the guy?" Malc asked.

"Yes."

"Okay. Here we go."

Grainy CCTV videos of gray London streets began to fill the screens, all moving at different speeds. My eyes darted between them all, until one began to flash.

"Aha!" Malc clicked on a series of things on his laptop, and the video expanded across multiple monitors.

"It's Alex." I watched as he sauntered down the street, looking left and right as he went.

"This is the road around the corner from the spa, the day the page went missing."

I let out a long breath. "So it was him. I was right."

Malc glanced at me, then the video began to speed up. "Let's see how long it took him to pull off the heist," he muttered. A couple moments later, he paused it again.

There, amidst three or four other pedestrians, was Alex, heading back the way he came, hands in his jean pockets. "An hour and eight minutes," announced Malc, putting the two stills side by side and pointing at the timestamps.

"Okay. So, what does that tell us?" Rory was staring at the images. "He's alone. Which is a shame."

"Yeah." It was a shame. If he'd had an accomplice we would have had a lead. "Malc, did you say there was nothing on the CCTV from the neighborhood he lived in?"

"No. Checked it all. No sign of anyone entering the building after him, other than two other people who lived on the block, until the Ward arrived."

As if to prove it, another video flashed up on the screen. It showed Banks heading toward the tower block, from the vantage-point of a high camera.

"Banks arrived on his own?"

"Yeah. First on the scene."

"But... But Malc, we were listening when someone radioed it in to him. Remember? They asked for someone experienced, and then Banks was patched through."

"So?"

"So wouldn't someone have had to go there first to report it? When we saw him at the crime scene, Nox said he couldn't feel the magical signature, and Banks told him something about sprites who check all magical murders within moments. That sprite must have been there first."

"A sprite might not need to enter the same way. They could get into the apartment by magic," Rory said. "Or they may not show up on cameras. Depends on the sprite."

"Oh." My shoulders deflated. I thought I'd had something there. Not that it would have been a good thing if a respected magical policeman was the killer. Especially as he was the one currently questioning Nox.

I stared glumly at the still footage on the TV screens, eyes wandering absently over the grimy streets that housed buildings like Scared Sleep Spa. There was a shop named Bargain Electricals, a homeless guy sitting in the recessed doorway with a hat in front of him to collect coins from passersby.

I leaned forward as something took my attention. His eyes. The guy's eyes were fixed on the figure of Alex, despite there being multiple other people around.

"Malc, zoom in on that guy in the doorway."

"The homeless guy?"

"Yes."

He did, and Rory stepped forward. "And zoom in on the image of Banks outside Alex's flat," she said, gripping the back of Malc's chair as I leaned farther forward.

Malc moved the blown-up image of the homeless guy next to the zoomed-in picture of Banks.

"Fuck," Rory breathed, and my heart stammered in my chest. "It's him."

THIRTY-FIVE

BETH

"Oh, shit," said Malc, staring at the pictures. They were bad quality, but there was no question. The homeless guy was Banks.

"He was watching Alex. Does that mean he knew about the theft?"

"He must have. But what about the footage of him at Alex's?"

Malc turned excitedly to us. "He could have paid or blackmailed a sprite into saying there had been a murder with a big magical signature, waited for it to be radio'd into him, then killed Alex when he got there."

I stared at him. "So when we heard it on the radio... Alex was still alive? And Banks killed him moments later, when he arrived at the apartment?"

"That's a hell of a risk," Rory said. "What if the dispatcher had given it to another officer, instead of him?"

Malc pulled a face. "If there's a big magical signature

and lots of blood, then they're calling Banks in. Everyone in London knows that. Well, everyone connected to the Ward, anyway."

"Well, what if someone else had got there before him?"

"If he was close by, then he'd have had time before anyone else arrived. It wouldn't take long to kill Alex and take the page."

I laid my sweating palms flat on the desk and stared at the footage.

It fit. It all fit. And now, the killer had Nox.

"What do we do now? What power does Banks have?" I asked, realizing the question had never come up. "What is he?"

"Angel."

"Great," I said, lifting my hands and putting my head in them. "Course he is."

"With the backing of the entire Ward, a load of planted evidence against the Boss, and possibly a sprite on his payroll," reeled off Malc.

"Fuck," said Rory, for the second time.

"Any ideas?" I said, looking between them, still squeezing my temples.

Neither spoke.

"We're going to have to go in there. Nox is allowed visitors, right?"

"I don't know."

"Well, I don't care. We'll go there, and we'll make Banks confess. Malc, you can hack Ward shit, right?"

Malc blinked his red eyes at me. "I can hack their radios."

"So, if I can get him to confess with a radio on, can you record it?"

"Erm, yeah." He spun back to his laptop. "The only problem would be knowing what radio, and when. But..." His eyes whizzed over his screen as he moved the mouse lightning fast. "I'll need ten minutes to get the recording software fully set up, but I think I can record *all* of the frequencies. If I record everything, that should cover it?"

I nodded. "Yes. Record everything. Even if we have to go through hours of tape afterward to find it, we'll have it."

"I'm on it, Girl Boss." He gave me a salute, and started typing furiously. I opted to ignore the term Girl Boss, and turned to Rory.

"Where are they questioning Nox?"

"Ward HQ."

"Let's go."

Claude pulled the car up just off Trafalgar Square, and my eyes lingered on the huge lion statues as we crawled past them to our stop. There were lots of streets leading off the iconic square, and when I got out of the car, I found myself on the opposite side from the National Gallery, in a street dominated by five- or six-story rows of what would once have been houses, now been repurposed as offices, on one side, and bars

and tourist shops on the ground floor of the other. A row of
Canadian flags flew from the front of the building next to us,
impressive white-stone columns breaking up the glass front
of what I assumed was the Canadian Embassy.

"Good luck, Miss Abbott," said Claude sincerely.

"Thanks, Claude."

Rory strode past me to the recessed entrance of the
building next to the Embassy. Fraud Office read a sign on
the door, on a faded metal plate.

She pushed open the door, and I followed her
through.

A decent sized lobby was beyond, and a smiling
woman with her hair in a neat bun greeted us, holding an
iPad. Beyond her, at the back of the room, were three
elevators and a guard scrolling through his phone.

"How can I help you today?"

She directed the question at Rory, so I knew immediately that she was magical.

"We're here to see Mr. Nox."

The woman's smile slipped fractionally. "Oh. Okay. I
don't believe we were expecting visitors for Mr. Nox."

"We have important information, regarding his
arrest," I said. "We have to pass it over to Banks."

"Mr. Nox hasn't been arrested," she said. "He's just
being questioned. Along with eight other potential
felons." She gave us another smile, this one weary. "It's
busy here today."

Rory tapped her foot on the shiny wooden floor, and
folded her arms. "Lucifer Morningstar, keeper of sins,

and punisher of evil, has visitors," she growled. "Please let him know. Now."

A bolt of envy at the way the woman instantly started pressing buttons on her iPad, punctuated by nervous glances at Rory, whizzed through my gut.

I didn't want to be as grumpy as the pixie, but man, could I use some of her authority.

I was going to need it, if we were about to face off with Banks. Nerves made my skin prickle. I was hoping against hope that we would be able to see Nox and Banks together. If we ended up alone with Banks, we could be in trouble.

Rory has magic, and an attitude, I reminded myself. We'd be fine.

We just needed to get Banks to admit to the killing, with his radio on.

I swallowed, the action difficult because my throat was so dry.

I'd spent the entire thirty minute drive to Ward HQ trying to work out how the hell I was going to get Banks to turn on his radio, and leave it on.

So far, I'd come up with nothing.

"Go on up to floor four," the woman said, looking up from her tablet. "Warden Banks will meet you."

My stomach was turning somersaults as we got into the elevator. My eyes had snagged on the guard's radio as we had passed him, and now my mind was whirring. Banks wouldn't be the only one with a radio. There would be loads in the building, surely? And Malc was recording them all.

Rory didn't speak on the short ride up, just glared at the small camera in the top corner of the elevator, while I shifted anxiously from one foot to the other.

"Ladies," came Banks calm voice as the elevator pinged and the doors slid open. "Thank you for visiting. I'm informed that you have something to share with me?"

"Where's Nox?" I demanded as we stepped out of the elevator. The forcefulness of my own voice startled me, but the second I saw Bank's face, anger filled me. I felt a weird swirling in my chest, squarely under my ribs. It was a burning ball of fury that someone would mess with Nox's life, with my life, and think they could get away with it.

It wasn't me, it was Nox's power, but I was sure as hell going to use it.

"Mr. Nox is detained. He is refusing to co-operate."

A sound that might actually have been a snarl escaped my lips. "I want to see him."

"That's not possible."

"Then I'll tell you nothing." I channeled Rory and crossed my arms over my chest. Banks looked between me and the pixie and sighed.

"This way." He began to walk down the hallway and we followed. It looked like the sort of corridor you'd find in a school or hospital, nothing remotely magical about it. I eyed the radio on Banks' hip. There had to be a way to get it off him. Or maybe I could distract him and Rory could find another one?

I looked sideways at her, wondering if I could get a

message to her. She met my eyes for a moment and then focused ahead again.

Banks stopped, pushing open the handle of one of many plain wooden doors along the corridor. He gestured for us to go ahead, and a trickle of trepidation rolled down my spine. Could it be a trap?

It wasn't like we had much choice. And the woman with the iPad knew we were there.

I stepped through.

The place no longer felt like a school or a hospital. I tried to keep my eyes from giving away my shock.

It was as though I'd walked into the Iron Age. I'd been expecting a plainly decorated office room with a table, or maybe an interview room like on police shows. I had not expected the freaking dungeon from a castle.

I looked sharply at Rory, who didn't seem fazed in the slightest.

The stone floor was covered in straw, and small metal stools and a bucket stood on the far side of the room. The walls were stone too, and there were no windows, just low light from the iron candle sconces on the wall.

"Where's Nox?" I ground out.

Banks leaned over and pressed down on an iron swirly shape that I had assumed to be an empty sconce. The wall to my left shimmered and turned completely transparent, showing us the room next door.

Nox knelt on the straw-covered stone, shirtless, his wings spread all the way to each side of the tiny room, and his hands tied behind his back.

Rage flooded me, hot and hard and instant. "Let him go!"

"If he had co-operated, then-"

I didn't hear the rest of what Banks said, because Nox looked up and saw us through the now invisible wall.

He roared, the sound only just audible, leapt to his feet, and launched himself at us. His shoulder slammed off the barrier the wall was still creating, and he staggered backward. His eyes were inky black, and shadows billowed out across his gleaming wings.

Banks reached out and pulled down on another part of the iron sconce.

"There. He can hear us now, but I've turned his microphone off."

Anger was coursing through me, and I found myself opening and closing my mouth furiously as I stared at the lethal beauty contained before me.

If I said a word about Banks being the killer before we could record it, I'd blow any chance of clearing Nox's name. And worse, we would show our hand.

"How are you keeping him in there?" I spat.

"Magical restraints," said Rory, her tone quiet and hard. She was pissed too. "They're only supposed to be used in extreme cases."

"Mr. Nox is an extreme case. He is one of the most powerful free beings in London."

"He's one of the most powerful beings in the world," I snapped, not even realizing I'd said it. "Let him go, now."

"No. I have reason to believe he killed your ex-boyfriend in a fit of jealously." Banks' cool eyes locked on mine, and the rage under my ribs roared to life.

"You think you can-" I started, but Rory stepped up between us, and shoved Banks in the chest. He took a small step back, the force doing little to him.

"Physical abuse of a Warden is a punishable offense," he told her calmly.

"Oh yeah? I'd better do it properly then," she said. Before I had time to register what was happening, her fist darted out and into Banks' nose. He cried out, and quick as a flash, she yanked his radio from the belt on his hip.

For a brief second, I thought she'd got it, but his hand slammed down over hers, and for the first time, the calm was gone from his expression.

"What the hell do you want with this?" he asked, yanking the radio out, and pulling Rory's arm hard with it. Blood was starting to drip from his nose.

Rory said nothing, just glowered at him.

Still staring at her, Banks pressed the button on the radio. "One more to detain, please Cheryl. GBH."

"Righto, Sir," came the crackled reply. "I'll be there in three minutes."

Nox banged on the see-through wall, making me start, and Banks turned to face him. He kept Rory's arm in his grip, but the hand holding radio fell lax to his side.

Nox had maneuvered his bound wrists to his front, and had them pressed against the clear wall. His face wore an expression of pure hatred, and the power inside me responded, churning angrily.

This guy was going down. He was a killer, and a liar.

And he had the Sloth page.

The other officer was coming in three minutes. Maybe I didn't need the radio after all. Maybe I could get him to say the wrong thing when the other Warden was present?

I needed to rattle him.

Taking a deep breath, I committed. "Where did you hide the Sloth page? You know, once you took it from Alex's dead body. After you killed him."

Bank's eyes turned granite. "Your new boyfriend killed your last one, little girl. And you shouldn't really be surprised. The devil hardly carries a good reputation."

"Nox doesn't kill for greed. Which is what I suspect motivated you. You wanted the Sloth page. Why?"

My words came out a little thick, but the new burning power inside my core kept them steady as Banks advanced on me, throwing Rory's wrist away.

A weird, tingly feeling rolled over me as he got close, and I heard Nox banging on the wall again.

I kept my eyes on Banks, only breaking his stare for a split second to check the radio was still in his hand.

"One of Lucifer's feathers was found in your ex's flat. Because Lucifer left it there when he killed him."

"That's a good point," I said, thrusting out my chin. My heart was pounding now, my pulse racing. But I was no longer sure it was being caused by fear.

To my surprise, there was a thrill in knowing that I might best this powerful man. And even more exciting, that I might be the one to rescue Nox for once. "How did you get a feather? We know that you paid a sprite to radio in the fake murder. And we know that when you got to Alex's apartment, you committed the murder that had just been reported, and took the Sloth page that he had had stolen the previous week. But we don't know where you got the feather from."

The slight widening of his eyes and the twitch of his dark brows was enough to confirm that we'd got it right.

He was the killer. And he had the page.

THIRTY-SIX

BETH

"You're a bigger pain than I thought you would be," he growled, low so that only I could hear him. He took a step closer to me, so that there was only a foot between us. Instinct made me want to move back, but pride and rage kept me exactly where I was.

"Good. Give me the page. Let Nox go."

A sneer took his lips, the blood from his cracked nose now dried onto his skin. Suddenly, he threw his left arm out. A screeching sound accompanied a whoosh of power, and a dull thud sounded. I looked away from his face long enough to see that Rory had managed to get the door open, but now she was pinned against the wall next to it by a shining yellow force of some sort. She looked like she was in the middle of swearing at him, but her face was immobile.

A frisson of fear made its way through me, jostling with the adrenaline. If he could disable Rory so easily.... And I was a freaking kitten next to her.

"Well, Miss Abbott. Looks like I'll have to send you down with the devil. As you've gleaned so much."

"Sir?"

A woman stepped through the door, wearing a uniform and a confused frown. She had dark skin and black hair tight in a bun, and she slowly removed a baton from her belt as she looked between Banks standing menacingly over me, and Rory pinned to the wall by magic. Then her eyes fell on Nox on the other side of the barrier.

Murder was in his eyes.

"Sir, what the fuck is going on?"

"Take her," Banks said, gesturing to Rory. The force-field vanished and she fell to her knees.

"Lying, two-faced, treacherous bag of shit," Rory gasped.

"Banks killed Alex," I said as fast as could to the woman. "Not Nox." She looked at me skeptically, and Banks turned to smile at her.

"Apparently I'm a murderer and a thief." He looked pointedly at Nox. Who, to be completely fair, looked significantly more like he was capable of ripping someone's throat out at that moment than Banks did.

"It's true. If you search him right now, I believe you'll find the sin page for the power of Sloth." Banks stiffened, ever so slightly, and my pulse rocketed.

It was true. He definitely had the page on him. I'd been making a blind punt, hoping that he believed the only safe place for something so valuable would be on his person.

"Please." I turned up the emotion in my voice as I stared at the Warden. "Please, just search him. You'll see I'm right. And if I'm not you were just doing your job."

I saw a flicker of doubt in the woman's brown eyes as she looked from Rory, still heaving in air on her hands and knees, to Nox, shirtless and restrained.

"Sir? This does go beyond normal protocol..." She gestured a the two of them.

"Lucifer does not come under the same rules as the others!" Banks barked. "He's ten times more powerful than anyone else in this building, and I will restrain him as I see fit."

All the calm I'd seen as his signature had gone, and clearly the Warden wasn't used to seeing him like this either. She took a tiny step backward and squared her shoulders.

"It can't hurt for you to turn out your pockets, sir," she said.

I flicked my eyes down her uniform, looking for a radio. It was on her right hip, the opposite side to where Rory knelt on the floor.

Frustration welled inside me. "Turn on your radio," I spluttered.

She frowned at me. "Why?"

A low laugh came from Banks. "That's why you wanted the radio? You wanted our conversation to be broadcast to someone?"

I glared at the other Warden, willing her to turn the damn thing on. But she just stared at Banks in confusion. "Sir, are you okay?"

His laugh petered out. He flicked a hand and the door slammed closed behind the woman. "Just fine, thank you, Cheryl. Now, you were questioning my loyalty to the Ward and suggesting that I was a criminal?"

"What? No, I just asked if you could turn out your pockets."

"And why would you want me to do that? Unless you believed this human scum might be telling you the truth about me being a murderer?" There was a sickly sweet tone to his voice, laced with danger. Cheryl felt it too. She took another step back, the look on her face utter confusion.

"Sir, I don't understand. You would be the first to make sure we followed procedure and checked all leads."

"Even when they impugn my integrity? No, Cheryl. I am beyond judgement."

"Nobody is beyond judgement. You killed Alex, and you'll sure as fuck be judged for it," I said. I needed him to admit to it, in front of a Warden.

Banks let out a long breath, then turned back to me. "You are beyond irritating." He raised his hand and yellow energy balled in front of his palm. At the same time Nox banged on the wall, pain exploded in every cell of my body. I couldn't help the scream, and black rushed my vision as all my muscles began to spasm.

I vaguely heard Rory shout and Cheryl's cries before my body fell limp. The pain ebbed away, and the next feeling I was aware of was all of my left side hitting cool, hard stone.

I rolled, sweat covering me, air hard to breathe in.

The fire in my chest flared, and my lungs seemed to expand, sucking in what I needed to clear my head.

"Banks, this is unacceptable!" Cheryl was shouting, then her words cut off with a gurgle.

I pushed myself to a sitting position, my skin tingling like I'd been electrocuted. Rory was in a heap by the door, motionless, and Cheryl was slumped on the ground, apparently unconscious. I watched Rory until I was sure her chest was moving, before looking at Nox. He was hammering on the wall, flames licking over his pounding fists and dancing up his forearms.

"Well, you've royally fucked this up for me," hissed Banks, turning on me. "You and that fucking pixie will have to become Nox's next victims. And it's your own damned fault. I wasn't supposed to kill you, but you've left me no fucking choice."

"Why weren't you supposed to kill me?" It probably wasn't the right question, but it was the one that tumbled thickly from my numb lips.

"Leverage." His eyes gleamed with cruelty and he crouched down in front of me. The radio was gone from his hand. Not that it mattered any more. Either we were getting out of here alive with Cheryl as a witness that Banks was a murderous asshole, or he would kill us. I couldn't see any other outcomes.

"Leverage?"

"Indeed."

Power tugged at my body, and I found myself lifted into the air. Banks grinned as swished his hand, and I spun around like I was in some sort of display case.

Heat pulsed through me, caused by the power in my chest. Could I access it?

I spun again, this time vertically. My hair fell down my face as my feet rose, heat flooding my cheeks, and my stomach churning. Banks didn't halt my movement until I was completely upside-down. The contents of my jacket pockets clattered to the ground, and Banks's eyes flicked to the stone floor.

"This has power," he muttered, and stooped to pick something up.

I windmilled my arms, trying to right myself, but I stayed exactly where I was, my torso immobile.

I moved my head, trying to see what he had picked up.

Gabriel's turtle trinket.

"What is this?"

I rose in the air, still upside down, until my face was level with his. My feet were almost touching the stone ceiling.

He held up the turtle and pushed his face menacingly at mine.

I summoned up all my courage, channeled Rory's take-no-shit attitude, and head-butted him.

I heard his nose crack as he stumbled backward, and instead of the sound making me feel unwell, I felt a burst of pride.

"Fuck you." My words were barely audible through his own swearing, but I heard myself say them, and a slim smile crossed my face.

I wasn't going down without a fight, even if I was alone.

Pain crashed through the side of my head as he hit me.

There was a primal roar from the other side of the wall, and the magic holding me up vanished. I barely had time or the presence of mind to lift my head and curl my arms around it defensively, ensuring I didn't crack my skull open as I landed.

My shoulder took the brunt of my five foot fall. For a second I thought I was going to throw up, stars clouding my vision entirely as agony swallowed me whole.

"Lucifer! Can you hear me? I'm going to make her suffer, Lucifer."

Nox bellowed again, the sound grounding me. I was sprawled on my front, pain surging through my right side. I moved my left arm, groping forward, trying to push myself up.

Banks crouched down over me, and yanked me up by the back of my neck.

Fresh agony shot through my shoulder, and I only managed a half-assed swipe with my left arm.

He held the turtle up in front of me again. "What is this? Do I need it for the sins? Tell me!" He shook me, and I tried desperately to make my brain work. Why was he so interested in the trinket? He seemed to think it was something to do with Nox - Gabriel was Nox's brother. Were his senses mixing the brother's powers up?

Gabriel... The angel's conversation with me

hammered into my head as I stared glassily at the tiny turtle.

If you need me, or if I can help him, use this.

That's what Gabriel had said. Nox was locked away, his power restricted. Rory was unconscious, and I didn't have the magic to beat the murderous angel holding me up by the scruff, as though I were some kind of animal.

With a desperate surge of energy, I threw my left hand up and closed it over Banks', and the turtle.

"Gabriel," I gasped, and prayed to any of the crazy freaking gods these guys answered to that it worked.

THIRTY-SEVEN

BETH

Banks' face flashed with anger, and he threw me backward. I landed on my ass, which was a mercy, as my shoulder couldn't take another hit, and my hip was screaming in pain too.

I drew in air, trying to steady my swimming head. I realized hazily that Nox's banging had stopped, and I turned to him. He was as still as stone, his furious gaze just as hard and fixed on Banks.

"What the fuck did you just do?" snarled Banks, but I didn't answer him. I didn't even look at him.

I wasn't sure if I had done anything at all.

"Nox!" I tried to shout, but my lips felt wrong.

He must have heard me. Those granite eyes turned on me, and his wings snapped out taut behind him. Fire roared to life along his chest, and the blackness of his eyes burst to life with fire.

A clap of thunder filled the room, and my body

convulsed in surprise. It sent new waves of pain through me, bile rising in my throat.

Banks moved to me, fast, as though he knew what was coming. But as he swiped a large fist down toward me, a cool summer breeze filled my nose, and suddenly he was swept of his feet, flying backward.

He landed on the stone, skidding toward the crumpled form of Cheryl.

There was a flicker of bright white light, and Gabriel appeared in the center of the room.

He turned in a circle, taking in me, Nox, and the two unconscious women. Then he looked at Banks again.

"He killed Alex. Because Alex stole Sloth's page. He planted Nox's feather there." My words were a slur.

Gabriel stalked forward.

"Lies. All lies," Banks said, struggling to his feet.

Gabriel held out his hand, and Bank's uniform began to glow. With a flick, all the items on his person flew off in a stream. His radio, a cellphone, a packet of mints, the buckle of his belt... a small plastic tube. Gabriel moved his hand again, and the myriad of items fell to the floor.

Panic clouded Bank's face. Gabriel turned, dropping into a crouch next to me. He touched my face, and a bang on the wall accompanied a flash of intense heat that flooded my body.

Everything darkened for a long second, but when I opened my eyes my vision had cleared completely. Gabriel straightened, and advanced on Banks.

The pain in my shoulder and hip was gone.

Completely. I flexed my right arm. When I felt nothing, I leaped to my feet.

"Let Nox out!" I shouted at Gabriel.

"No. He will choose the wrong punishment." They were the only words Gabriel had uttered. I looked at Nox, beating on the wall, lethal fury in his every movement.

He might be right, I realized.

I looked at Banks, who was furiously backing up, looking between Nox and Gabriel.

"I believe you fucked with the wrong angels," I found myself saying.

He dropped down abruptly, grabbing the fallen form of Cheryl. "Stop, or I'll kill her."

Gabriel stopped moving as Banks hauled her up, wrapping a hand around her throat as her head hung limp.

Nox continued to pound.

Crackling energy filled the room, yellow flashes zipping around, stinging my skin.

"Don't even think about it, Banks," said Gabriel. There was a flash of light, a spike of electricity in the air, and he and Cheryl were gone.

The pounding stopped.

"What happened?"

"He's stronger than I thought he was. He left this realm."

Gabriel ducked down and touched Rory's cheek. She jerked a little, then her eyelids fluttered.

"Let Nox out, please."

Gabriel glanced up at the fierce winged form in the next room, then looked at me. "The keys are there." He pointed to the pile of Banks' stuff. "I'm going nowhere near my brother in that state. I believe you might be the only person he won't kill right now."

With a tiny smile, he straightened, and vanished with a gust of ocean breeze.

I dove for the small ring of keys on the floor, feeling only a tiny stab of guilt for ignoring Rory's mumbling as she came to.

I darted from the room, half sprinting to the next door.

I got the right key on the second try, yanked down the handle, and threw open the door to Nox's cell.

Heat slammed into me, and then Nox was there, filling my vision.

"Beth," he hissed, then he was ducking his head, his mouth claiming mine in a kiss fiercer than I'd ever experienced.

He moved, leaving me gasping for air. "I will kill him, Beth. I will fucking kill him."

I dragged my eyes over him, looking for injuries, and I could see the same in his roving gaze. He was checking every inch of me, drinking my presence in.

His hands were still bound, but other than that he looked strong and well. Too well. His muscles were bulging, power throbbing from him.

He was ready to fight.

"Nox, I... I was so worried."

The fierceness ebbed just a fraction. "You fought back, Beth. You were fucking magnificent."

"Magnificent? I head-butted him."

"He hurt you. I will tear him limb from fucking limb." He had become almost primal, his words short, his usual eloquence vanished. "You called my brother." Nox's eyes darkened, his already tense body stiffening further.

I heard noise in the corridor behind me, and Rory's clipped, angry voice.

"Yes. He gave me that turtle trinket when he came to the park. Before the hellhound."

"I owe him now." His tone made it clear that this was not tolerable.

"No, *I* owe him."

"Never," Nox snarled. Flames sparked on his curled fists. "You will owe nothing to anyone but me. You will *be* nothing to anyone but me. Ever."

I reached up and touched his cheek. "I'll never ask your brother for help again," I said. "Unless it's literally the only way to save all our lives."

Anger flickered over his face. "My life was not in danger. But yours may have been." Light flared in his eyes, chasing away some of the darkness. "Perhaps your decision was necessary."

I thought so, too. Not least because Gabriel appeared to have completely healed me. But I thought it best not to mention that, remembering Nox's roar when Gabriel had touched me.

.   .   .

There was a loud knock, and I turned to see Rory standing next to two Wardens.

"Mr. Nox," one of them said, lifting a small pocketknife. He thrust his bound wrists at her, and she flinched.

"Gabriel spoke with the Ward. They're coordinating with the other realms to look for Banks," Rory said.

"He'd better hope they find him before I do," Nox snarled. The woman had just been about the cut the bindings when fire flared to life on his skin, and she yanked her hand back.

I held my hand out to her, an offer to take the knife. She turned it over to me with a grateful smile and scurried back to the door.

The knife was icy cold, pulsing with magical energy. Nox's flames died instantly as I moved close, and I cut the rope. As soon as it fell to the floor Nox glowered at it, and it burst into flame.

"Shame you couldn't do that when it was on you, huh?"

Nox ignored my words, instead reaching out and pulling me tight to his chest. His fingers laced into my hair, and he pressed as much of my body to his as he could without hurting me.

His display surprised me, given that there were three other people in the room. But I snaked my arms around him, his solid heat making my heart swell.

"You rescued me," he said, moving so that he could look down at me. His thumb stroked down my cheek.

I opened my mouth to tell him that technically his brother rescued him, but he kissed me before I could speak. Which was definitely a good thing.

Rory coughed. "When you guys are done, I've got something you're going to want to look at."

We both turned to her, and she held up the plastic tube that had been in Nox's uniform.

She unscrewed the cap, and tipped it up. A tightly rolled scroll slid out and she unrolled it before reaching out to pass it to Nox. Keeping one arm tight around me, he took the scroll from her.

I stared at the words.

Quod acedia est peccatum Quintus potestate.

Non MINORIS carnis otiosa.

Non discount nonnumquam ignoratur a causa malum in auxilium.

Non ignorare nihil crudelitatis.

Acedia vero est in potentia multus et fortis: et hic habes eius, tenetur ad Dominum Sin.

"What does it say?"

.   .   .

"The fifth sin is the power of Sloth.

Do not underestimate the sinful nature of idleness.

Do not discount the inherent evil in ignoring a plea for help.

Do not ignore the cruelty in doing nothing.

The power of Sloth is vast and mighty, and here you find it, bound to the Lord of Sin."

I blew out a breath. "It's the Sloth page."

"Yes."

THIRTY-EIGHT

NOX

"Bring Sloth to me," I barked. Impotent rage was still crashing through my body, and the only thing keeping it at bay was Beth's presence beside me.

"Here?" asked Rory.

"No. My office."

"Claude is outside."

"You take the car." I looked down at Beth, drinking in her beautiful face. When I'd watched Banks strike her, able to do nothing.... My voice was raw and low, and I made sure only she could hear me. "I have been bound and restrained, and I need to fly. Will you join me?"

She nodded. "Always."

She didn't say a word as we soared over London, just pressed her face to my neck and held me tight.

I held her tighter.

Watching her with Banks, utterly unable to protect

her, had fired something in me that I didn't know was possible for a fallen angel.

It wasn't lust, driving a need for her physically, and it wasn't pride, wanting to protect or her, and it wasn't greed, wanting to own her.

It was something that had no connection to the sins. Something primal. Something soulful.

It was love.

The devil should not be capable of love.

I had been created to punish, not love. I had been brought into the world to contain massive power, to terrorize and torture. Not protect and nurture.

Beth moved in my arms, and I felt her pounding heart against my own chest.

I needed to own that heart. I needed it as much as I needed my magic to live.

The memory of my brother touching her face so tenderly lanced through my head, and my lip curled.

He may have come to her rescue, but I didn't trust the bastard.

We were now in his debt, and the devil was indebted to nobody.

I banked, turning up my speed, trying to blast away the rage that had built up so ferociously inside me, only to be left unspent.

The cold air sliced through my feathers, and Beth squeezed me tighter.

"I'm yours, Nox."

I only just heard her voice, over the rushing wind. My body rose, taking us higher, my wings beating delightedly in response to those three words.

"And I am yours," I answered.

Her lips were hot against my skin when she pressed a solitary kiss on my neck.

It was what I had needed. A clarity swept through me, the anger and doubt shimmying away from its brightness, receding to darker corners of my mind.

The power of Sloth had been found.

Next, I would get Pride and Envy. I would work out what to do with Wrath. I would find the damned book.

And I would find a way to end Examinus' hold on me. It was the only way I could share a life with Beth that she could enjoy. I couldn't have her standing at my side in hell, exposed to the worst of conscious nature. I wished that life on nobody.

When I was at full power, I would use it to find a way to make her happy. For the rest of her life.

THIRTY-NINE

BETH

"Oh man, am I glad you found it." Sloth was slumped in a wheelchair in Nox's office and he stank of stale sweat and old food. I took a step further away from him, and Rory followed suit.

Nox held up the page, giving him a disgusted look. "I don't know if your body will survive, once you have had the power of Sloth removed."

I stiffened at Nox's words. I was getting braver, but I was not ready to watch somebody die.

"I will do my best to save you."

Sloth just shrugged. "I don't care anymore."

Nox shook his head. "Fucking Sloth," he muttered. "I fucking hate this sin."

"You and me both, man," he agreed.

Nox was still shirtless, and with a small flex of his chest, his wings unfurled from behind him. He held up the page and began to read.

As he said the words, in Latin, a faint glimmer appeared around Sloth. His eyes slipped shut.

Shadows burst out of the fallen angel's ruined body, turning and twisting like a tornado in the middle of the office. Nox clapped his hands together with a boom, and when he parted them they were filled light the same color as the blue of his eyes. The shadowy hurricane was drawn to the light like a magnet, rushing toward it.

Nox let out a hiss as the shadows were sucked into the light, and I stared as a second later I saw the dark shapes spread across his wings, edging the gleaming feathers before melting into the gold.

The light died away to nothing, and Sloth slumped forward in his chair.

Rory stepped closer to him, a reluctant look on her face. Her pink magic swelled up out of her palms and hovered before him.

"He's alive. Just."

"Good."

Nox picked up his phone. "You can have him now."

The door opened, and two uniformed Wardens wheeled Sloth's prone form out of the room.

I let out a sigh of relief and turned to Nox. "So? How do you feel? Any more powerful?"

"It's a shite power," he grumbled.

"But it is a power," I said. "And two days ago, we were no closer to getting any of them back."

He gave me a wan smile. "Where has your optimism been all my life?"

"On hold, waiting to cheer up the devil, apparently."

"If you want to cheer me up, I can think of better ways."

"I'm leaving," said Rory. Neither of us looked at her.

"Thank you for your help, Rory," Nox said, his eyes stormy with desire.

"Whatever," she answered.

I moved toward Nox, my body tingling in anticipation.

We wouldn't sleep together. It was too risky. But maybe a little heavy petting wouldn't be so dangerous?

"Boss!" I halted at the sound of Malc's voice.

Nox's eyes broke from mine and dropped to the laptop on his desk.

"Boss, I think I got something you're going to want to hear."

"I'm busy, Malcolm," he growled down at his laptop. I moved to stand next to Nox, Malc's face appearing on the screen.

"Hi Malc." I gave him a small wave.

"Oh, good, you're already there. Boss, I just had to hack your laptop to get through to you. This is important. It's about Beth."

We both tensed, I leaned closer to the screen. "What about me?"

"You know how you told me to record all of the radios?"

"Yeah."

"Well, I did. And I overheard something you're going to find interesting. You ready?"

We both nodded, and a tinny voice played through the laptop.

"Look, at some point, she's going to start looking for her parents," said a male voice.

"Then you make sure she doesn't find a thing," replied a woman.

"Mr. Nox's hacker is pretty good ,you know. There's not a lot I can do. Especially if Michael gets involved."

"I don't care what Michael says. Make sure she finds nothing."

The transmission ended, and I heard Malc's voice as though it was very far away. Blood rushed in my ears, and I wondered if my heart had stopped beating completely.

"Beth? You okay? You're pale."

I felt Nox turn to me, then grip my shoulders. "Beth? What's wrong?"

"The woman," I stammered. "I know her voice. That's... That's my mom."

THE STORY CONTINUES IN WICKED HOPE.

THANKS FOR READING!

Thank you so much for reading Fallen Feathers, I hope you enjoyed it! If so I would be eternally grateful for a review! They help so much; just click here and leave a couple words, and you'll make my day :)

Printed in Great Britain
by Amazon

72696811R00158